"It Takes Everything I've Got Not To Touch You When I See You Sitting There Like That."

There was a long silence, and then her voice again. "Why don't you?"

Liam's jaw was flexed tight, his whole body tense, as he tried to hold back the desire for her that was building inside. "I didn't think it was a good idea. I'm your boss. We have to work together. Things would get weird. Wouldn't they?"

Please let her say no.

"I don't think so," she said, slowly climbing to her knees. "We're both adults. We know what this is and what it means." She crawled leisurely across the elevator floor, stopping in front of him. Her hands went to his belt buckle as she looked up at him through her thick, coal-black lashes. "What happens in the elevator stays in the elevator, right?"

Dear Reader,

I was so excited to be invited to participate in this great Harlequin Desire continuity. When I first learned about the Daughters of Power story line, I hoped that Liam and Francesca's book would be mine to write. My wish was granted!

I got to take two feuding executives who are too stubborn to acknowledge they're attracted to one another. Then, I trapped them in an elevator together on one of the hottest days of the year. As the temperature rises, clothes come off, sparks fly and the fun really begins. It's the perfect recipe for romance. *A* Very *Exclusive Engagement* features the handsome new ANS Network owner and his feisty vice president of community outreach in a situation they never anticipated—mandatory matrimony!

I hope you've enjoyed the fantastic stories of scandal and seduction in the Daughters of Power: The Capital as much as I have. If you like Liam and Francesca's story, tell me by visiting my website at www.andrealaurence.com, liking my fan page on Facebook or following me on Twitter. I love to hear from my readers!

Enjoy!

Andrea

ANDREA LAURENCE

A *VERY* EXCLUSIVE ENGAGEMENT

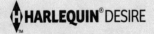

Special thanks and acknowledgment to Andrea Laurence for her contribution to the Daughters of Power: The Capital miniseries.

Recycling programs for this product may not exist in your area.

ISBN-13: 978-0-373-73241-8

A *VERY* EXCLUSIVE ENGAGEMENT

Printed in U.S.A.

HARLEQUIN®

www.Harlequin.com

Books by Andrea Laurence

Harlequin Desire

What Lies Beneath #2152
More Than He Expected #2172
*Undeniable Demands #2207
A Very *Exclusive Engagement* #2228

*Secrets of Eden

Other titles by this author available in ebook format.

ANDREA LAURENCE

has been a lover of reading and writing stories since she learned her ABCs. She always dreamed of seeing her work in print and is thrilled to finally be able to share her books with the world. A dedicated West Coast girl transplanted to the Deep South, she's working on her own "happily ever after" with her boyfriend and their collection of animals that shed like nobody's business. You can contact Andrea at her website, www.andrealaurence.com.

To my series mates—
Barbara, Michelle, Robyn, Rachel and Jennifer

It was a pleasure working with each of you.
Thanks for welcoming a newbie to the club.

And our editor, Charles

*Sei fantastico. È stato bello lavorare con voi.
Grazie per il cioccolato le sardine.*

One

Figlio di un allevatore di maiali.

Liam Crowe didn't speak Italian. The new owner of the American News Service network could barely order Italian food, and he was pretty sure his Executive Vice President of Community Outreach knew it.

Francesca Orr had muttered the words under her breath during today's emergency board meeting. He'd written down what she'd said—or at least a close enough approximation–in his notebook so he could look it up later. The words had fallen from her dark red lips in such a seductive way. Italian was a powerful language. You could order cheese and it would sound like a sincere declaration of love. Especially when spoken by the dark, exotic beauty who'd sat across the table from him.

And yet, he had the distinct impression that he wasn't going to like what she'd said to him.

He hadn't expected taking over the company from

Graham Boyle to be a cakewalk. The former owner and several employees were in jail following a phone-hacking scandal that had targeted the president of the United States. The first item on the agenda for the board meeting had been to suspend ANS reporter Angelica Pierce for suspicion of misconduct. Hayden Black was continuing his congressional investigation into the role Angelica may have played in the affair. Right now, they had enough cause for the suspension. When Black completed his investigation—and hopefully uncovered some hard evidence—Liam and his Board of Directors would determine what additional action to take.

He was walking into a corporate and political maelstrom, but that was the only reason he had been able to afford to buy controlling stock in the company in the first place. ANS was the crown jewel of broadcast media. The prize he'd always had his eye on. The backlash of the hacking scandal had brought the network and its owner, Graham Boyle, to their knees. Even with Graham behind bars and the network coming in last in the ratings for most time slots, Liam knew he couldn't pass up the opportunity to buy ANS.

So, they had a major scandal to overcome. A reputation to rebuild. Nothing in life was easy, and Liam liked a challenge. But he'd certainly hoped that the employees of ANS, and especially his own Board of Directors, would be supportive. From the night janitor to the CFO, jobs were on the line. Most of the people he spoke to were excited about him coming aboard and hopeful they could put the hacking scandal behind them to rebuild the network.

But not Francesca. It didn't make any sense. Sure, she had a rich and famous movie producer father to support her if she lost her position with ANS, but charity was her *job.* Surely she cared about the employees of the company as much as she cared about starving orphans and cancer patients.

It didn't seem like it, though. Francesca had sat at the conference room table in her formfitting flame-red suit and lit into him like she was the devil incarnate. Liam had been warned that she was a passionate and stubborn woman—that it wouldn't be personal if they bumped heads—but he wasn't prepared for this. The mere mention of streamlining the corporate budget to help absorb the losses had sent her on a tirade. But they simply couldn't throw millions at charitable causes when they were in such a tight financial position.

Suffice it to say, she disagreed.

With a sigh, Liam closed the lid on his briefcase and headed out of the executive conference room to find some lunch on his own. He'd planned to take some of the board members out, but everyone had scattered after the awkward meeting came to an end. He didn't blame them. Liam had managed to keep control of it, making sure they covered everything on the agenda, but it was a painful process.

Oddly enough, the only thing that had made it remotely tolerable for him was watching Francesca herself. In a room filled with older businesswomen and men in gray, black and navy suits, Francesca was the pop of color and life. Even when she wasn't speaking, his gaze kept straying back to her.

Her hair was ebony, flowing over her shoulders and curling down her back. Her almond-shaped eyes were dark brown with thick, black lashes. They were intriguing, even when narrowed at him in irritation. When she argued with him, color rushed to her face, giving her flawless tan skin a rosy undertone that seemed all the brighter for her fire-engine red suit and lipstick.

Liam typically had a thing for fiery, exotic women. He'd had his share of blond-haired, blue-eyed debutantes in private school but when he'd gone off to college, he found he had a taste for women a little bit spicier. Francesca, if she hadn't been trying to ruin his day and potentially his year, would've been just the kind of woman he'd ask out. But complicating this scenario with a fling gone wrong was something he didn't need.

Right now, what he *did* need was a stiff drink and some red meat from his favorite restaurant. He was glad ANS's corporate headquarters were in New York. While he loved his place in D.C., he liked coming back to his hometown. The best restaurants in the world, luxury box seats for his favorite baseball team…the vibe of Manhattan was just so different.

He'd be up here from time to time on business. Really, he wished it was all the time, but if he wanted to be in the thick of politics, which was ANS's focus, Washington was where he had to be. So he'd set up his main office in the D.C. newsroom, as Boyle had, keeping both his apartment in New York and the town house in Georgetown that he'd bought while he went to college there. It was the best of both worlds as far as he was concerned.

Liam went to his office before he left for lunch. He put his suitcase on the table and copied Francesca's words from his notebook onto a sticky note. He carried it with him, stopping at his assistant's desk on his way out.

"Jessica, it's finally over. Mrs. Banks will be bringing

you the paperwork to process Ms. Pierce's suspension. Human Resources needs to get that handled right way. Now that that mess is behind me, I think I'm going to find some lunch." He handed her the note with the Italian phrase written on it. "Could you get this translated for me while I'm gone? It's Italian."

Jessica smiled and nodded as though it wasn't an unusual request. She'd apparently done this in the past as Graham Boyle's assistant. "I'll take care of it, sir. I have the website bookmarked." Glancing down at the yellow paper she shook her head. "I see Ms. Orr has given you a special welcome to the company. This is one I haven't seen before."

"Should I feel honored?"

"I don't know yet, sir. I'll tell you once I look it up."

Liam chuckled, turning to leave, then stopping. "Out of curiosity," he asked, "what did she call Graham?"

"Her favorite was *stronzo*."

"What's that mean?"

"It has several translations, none of which I'm really comfortable saying out loud." Instead, she wrote them on the back of the note he'd handed her.

"Wow," he said, reading as she wrote. "Certainly not a pet name, then. I'm going to have to deal with Ms. Orr before this gets out of control."

A blur of red blew past him and he looked up to see Francesca heading for the elevators in a rush. "Here's my chance."

"Good luck, sir," he heard Jessica call to him as he trotted to the bank of elevators.

One of the doors had just opened and he watched Francesca step inside and turn to face him. She could see him coming. Their eyes met for a moment and then she reached to the panel to hit the button. To close the doors faster.

Nice.

He thrust his arm between the silver sliding panels and they reopened to allow him to join her. Francesca seemed less than pleased with the invasion. She eyeballed him for a moment under her dark lashes and then wrinkled her delicate nose as though he smelled of rotten fish. As the doors began to close again, she scooted into the far corner of the elevator even though they were alone in the car.

"We need to talk," Liam said as the car started moving down.

Francesca's eyes widened and her red lips tightened into a straight, hard line. "About what?" she asked innocently.

"About your attitude. I understand you're passionate about your work. But whether you like it or not, I'm in control of this company and I'm going to do whatever I have to do to save it from the mess that's been made of it. I'll not have you making a fool out of me in front of—"

Liam's words were cut off as the elevator lurched to a stop and the lights went out, blanketing them in total darkness.

This couldn't really be happening. She was not trapped in a broken elevator with Liam Crowe. Stubborn and ridiculously handsome Liam Crowe. But she should've known something bad was going to happen. There had been thirteen people sitting at the table during the board meeting. That was an omen of bad luck.

Nervously, she clutched at the gold Italian horn pendant around her neck and muttered a silent plea for good fortune. "What just happened?" she asked, her voice sounding smaller than she'd like, considering the blackout had interrupted a tongue lashing from her new boss.

"I don't know." They stood in the dark for a moment before the emergency lighting system kicked on and bathed them in red light. Liam walked over to the control panel and pulled out the phone that connected to the engineering room. Without saying anything, he hung it back up. Next, he hit the emergency button, but nothing happened; the entire panel was dark and unresponsive.

"Well?" Francesca asked.

"I think the power has gone out. The emergency phone is dead." He pulled his cell phone out and eyed the screen. "Do you have service on your phone? I don't."

She fished in her purse and retrieved her phone, shaking her head as she looked at the screen. There were no bars or internet connectivity. She never got good service in elevators, anyway. "Nothing."

"Damn it," Liam swore, putting his phone away. "I can't believe this."

"So what do we do now?"

Liam flopped back against the wall with a dull thud. "We wait. If the power outage is widespread, there's nothing anyone can do."

"So we just sit here?"

"Do you have a better suggestion? You were full of them this morning."

Francesca ignored his pointed words, crossed her arms defensively and turned away from him. She eyed the escape hatch in the ceiling. They could try to crawl out through there, but how high were they? They had started on the fifty-second floor and hadn't gone very far when the elevator stopped. They might be in between floors. Or the power could come back on while they were in the elevator shaft and they might get hurt. It probably was a better idea to sit it out.

The power would come back on at any moment. Hopefully.

"It's better to wait," she agreed reluctantly.

"I didn't think it was possible for us to agree on anything after the board meeting and that fit you threw."

Francesca turned on her heel to face him. "I did not throw a fit. I just wasn't docile enough to sit back like the others and let you make bad choices for the company. They're too scared to rock the boat."

"They're scared that the company can't bounce back from the scandal. And they didn't say anything because they know I'm right. We have to be fiscally responsible if we're going to—"

"Fiscally responsible? What about socially responsible? ANS has sponsored the Youth in Crisis charity gala for the past seven years. We can't just decide not to do it this year. It's only two weeks away. They count on that money to provide programs for at-risk teens. Those activities keep kids off the streets and involved in sports and create educational opportunities they wouldn't get without our money."

Liam frowned at her. She could see the firm set of his jaw even bathed in the dim red light. "You think I don't care about disadvantaged children?"

Francesca shrugged. "I don't know you well enough to say."

"Well, I do care," he snapped. "I personally attended the ball for the past two years and wrote a big fat check at both of them. But that's not the point. The point is we need to cut back on expenses to keep the company afloat until we can rebuild our image."

"No. You've got it backward," she insisted. "You need the charity events to rebuild your image so the company can stay afloat. What looks better in the midst of scandal than a company doing good deeds? It says to the public that some bad people did some bad things here, but the rest of us are committed to making things right. The advertisers will come flocking back."

Liam watched her for a moment, and she imagined the wheels turning in his head as he thought through her logic. "Your argument would've been a lot more effective if you hadn't shrieked and called me names in Italian."

Francesca frowned. She hadn't meant to lose her cool, but she couldn't help it. She had her mother's quick Italian tongue and her father's short fuse. It made for an explosive combination. "I have a bit of a temper," she said. "I get it from my father."

Anyone who had worked on the set of a Victor Orr film knew what could happen when things weren't going right. The large Irishman had a head of thick, black hair and a temper just as dark. He'd blow at a moment's notice and nothing short of her mother's soothing hand could calm him down. Francesca was just the same.

"Does he curse in Italian, too?"

"No, he doesn't speak a word of it and my mother likes it that way. My mother grew up in Sicily and met my father there when he was shooting a film. My mother's Italian heritage was always very important to her, so when I got older I spent summers there with my *nonna*."

"Nonna?"

"My maternal grandmother. I picked up a lot of Italian while I was there, including some key phrases I probably shouldn't know. I realized as a teenager that I could curse in Italian and my father wouldn't know what I was saying because he's Irish. From there it became a bad habit of mine. I'm sorry I yelled," she added. "I just care too much. I always have."

Francesca might take after her mother in most things, but her father had made his mark, as well. Victor Orr had come from poor beginnings and raised his two daughters not only to be grateful for what they had, but also to give to the less fortunate. All through high school, Francesca had volunteered at a soup kitchen on Saturdays. She'd organized charity canned food collections and blood drives at school. After college, her father helped her get an entry level job at ANS, where he was the largest minority stockholder. It hadn't taken long for her to work her way up to the head of community outreach. And she'd been good at it. Graham had never had room to complain about her doing anything less than a stellar job.

But it always came down to money. When things got tight, her budget was always the first to get cut. Why not eliminate some of the cushy corporate perks? Maybe slash the travel budget and force people to hold more teleconferences? Or cut back on the half gallon of hair gel the head anchor used each night for the evening news broadcast?

"I don't want to hack up your department," Liam said. "What you do is important for ANS and for the community. But I need a little give and take here. Everyone needs to tighten their belts. Not just you. But I need you to play along, too. It's hard enough to come into the leadership position of a company that's doing well, much less one like ANS. I'm going to do everything I can to get this network back on top, but I need everyone's support."

Francesca could hear the sincerity in his words. He did care about the company and its employees. They just didn't see eye to eye quite yet on what to do about it. She could convince him to see things her way eventually. She just had to take a page from her mother's playbook. It would take time and perhaps a softer hand than she had used with Graham. At least Liam seemed reasonable about it. That won him some points in her book. "Okay."

Liam looked at her for a moment, surveying her face as though he almost didn't believe his ears. Then he nodded. They stood silently in the elevator for a moment before Liam started shrugging out of his black suit coat. He tossed the expensive jacket to the ground and followed it with his silk tie. He unbuttoned his collar and took a deep breath, as if he had been unable to do it until then. "I'm glad we've called a truce because it's gotten too warm in here for me to fight anymore. Of course this had to happen on one of the hottest days of the year."

He was right. The air conditioning was off and it was in the high nineties today, which was unheard of in early May. The longer they sat in the elevator without air, the higher the temperature climbed.

Following his example, Francesca slipped out of her blazer, leaving her in a black silk and lace camisole and pencil skirt. Thank goodness she'd opted out of stockings today.

Kicking off her heels, she spread out her coat on the floor and sat down on it. She couldn't stand there in those pointy-toed stilettos any longer, and she'd given up hope for any immediate rescue. If they were going to be trapped in here for a while, she was going to be comfortable.

"I wish this had happened after lunch. Those bagels in the conference room burned off a long time ago."

Francesca knew exactly what he meant. She hadn't eaten since this morning. She'd had a cappuccino and a sweet *cornetto* before she'd left her hotel room, neither of which lasted very long. She typically ate a late lunch, so luckily she carried a few snacks in her purse.

Using the light of her phone, she started digging around in her bag. She found a granola bar, a pack of *Gocciole* Italian breakfast cookies and a bottle of water. "I have a few snacks with me. The question is whether we eat them now and hope we get let out soon, or whether we save them. It could be hours if it's a major blackout."

Liam slipped down to the floor across from her. "Now. Definitely now."

"You wouldn't last ten minutes on one of those survival reality shows."

"That's why I produce them and don't star in them. My idea of roughing it is having to eat in Times Square with the tourists. What do you have?"

"A peanut butter granola bar and some little Italian cookies. We can share the water."

"Which is your favorite?"

"I like the cookies. They're the kind my grandmother would feed me for breakfast when I stayed with her. They don't eat eggs or meat for breakfast like Americans do. It was one of the best parts of visiting her— cake and cookies for breakfast."

Liam grinned, and Francesca realized it was the first time she'd seen him smile. It was a shame. He had a beautiful smile that lit up his whole face. It seemed more natural than the serious expression he'd worn all day, as though he were normally a more carefree and relaxed kind of guy. The pressure of buying ANS must have been getting to him. He'd been all business this morning and her behavior certainly didn't help.

Now he was stressed out, hungry and irritated about being trapped in the elevator. She was glad she could make him smile, even if just for a moment. It made up for her behavior this morning. Maybe. She made a mental note to try to be more cordial in the future. He was being reasonable and there was no point in making things harder than they had to be.

"Cake for breakfast sounds awesome. As do summers in Italy. After high school I got to spend a week in Rome, but that's it. I didn't get around to seeing much more than the big sites like the Colosseum and the Parthenon." He looked down at the two packages in her hand. "I'll take the granola bar since you prefer the cookies. Thank you for sharing."

Francesca shrugged. "It's better than listening to your stomach growl for an hour." She tossed him the granola bar and opened the bottle of water to take a conservative sip.

Liam ripped into the packaging. His snack was gone before Francesca had even gotten the first cookie in her mouth. She chuckled as she ate a few, noting him eyeing her like a hungry tiger. Popping another into her mouth, she gently slung the open bag to him. "Here," she said. "I can't take you watching me like that."

"Are you sure?" he said, eyeing the cookies that were now in his hand.

"Yes. But when we get out of this elevator, you owe me."

"Agreed," he said, shoveling the first of several cookies into his mouth.

Francesca imagined it took a lot of food to keep a man Liam's size satisfied. He was big like her *nonno* had been. Her grandfather had died when she was only a few years old, but her *nonna* had told her about how much she had to cook for him after he worked a long shift. Like *Nonno,* Liam was more than six feet tall, solidly built but on the leaner side, as though he were a runner. A lot of people jogged around the National Mall in D.C. Or so she'd heard. She could imagine him down there with the others. Jogging shorts. No shirt. Sweat running down the hard muscles of his chest. It made her think maybe she should go down there every now and then, if just for the view.

She, however, didn't like to sweat. Running during the humid summers in Virginia was out of the question. As was running during the frigid, icy winters. So she just didn't. She watched what she ate, indulged when she really wanted to and walked as much as her heels would allow. That kept her at a trim but curvy weight that pleased her.

Speaking of sweating…she could feel the beads of sweat in her hairline, ready and waiting to start racing down the back of her neck. She already felt sticky, but there wasn't much else to take off unless she planned to get far closer to Liam than she ever intended.

Although that wouldn't be all bad.

It had been a while since Francesca had dated anyone. Her career had kept her busy, but she always kept her eyes open to the possibilities. Nothing of substance had popped up in a long time. But recently all of her friends seemed to be settling down. One by one, and she worried she might be the last.

Not that Liam Crowe was settling-down material. He was just sexy, fling material. She typically didn't indulge in pleasure without potential. But seeing those broad shoulders pulling against the confines of his shirt, she realized that he might be just what she needed. Something to release the pressure and give her the strength to hold out for "the one."

Francesca reached into her bag and pulled out a hair clip. She gathered up the thick, dark strands of her hair and twisted them up, securing them with the claw. It helped but only for a moment. Her tight-fitting pencil skirt was like a heavy, wet blanket thrown over her legs. And her camisole, while seemingly flimsy, was starting to get damp and cling to her skin.

If they didn't get out of this elevator soon, something had to come off. Taking another sip of water, she leaned her head back against the wall and counted herself lucky that if nothing else, she'd worn pretty, matching underwear today. She had the feeling that Liam would appreciate that.

Two

"Sweet mercy, it's hot!" Liam exclaimed, standing up. He felt as if he was being smothered by his crisp, starched dress shirt. He unfastened the buttons down the front and whipped it off with a sigh of relief. "I'm sorry if this makes you uncomfortable, but I've got to do it."

Francesca was sitting quietly in the corner and barely acknowledged him, although he did catch her opening her eyes slightly to catch a glimpse of him without his shirt on. She looked away a moment later, but it was enough to let him know she was curious. That was interesting.

He'd gotten a different insight into his feisty executive vice president of Community Outreach in the past two hours. He had a better understanding of her and what was important to her. Hopefully once they got out of this elevator they could work together without the animosity. And maybe they could be a little more than friendly. Once she had stopped yelling, he liked her. More than he probably should, considering that she worked for him.

"Francesca, take off some of your clothes. I know you're dying over there."

She shook her head adamantly, although he could see the beads of sweat running down her chest and into the valley between her breasts. "No, I'm fine."

"The hell you are. You're just as miserable as I am. That tank you're wearing looks like it will cover up enough to protect your honor. The skirt looks terribly clingy. Take it off. Really. I'm about ten minutes from losing these pants, so you might as well give up on any modesty left between us."

Francesca looked up at him with wide eyes. "Your pants?" she said, swallowing hard. Her gaze drifted down his bare chest to his belt and then lower.

"Yes. It's gotta be ninety-five degrees and climbing in this oven they call an elevator. You don't have to look at me, but I've got to do it. You might as well do it, too."

With a sigh of resignation, Francesca got up from the floor and started fussing with the latch on the back of her skirt. "I can't get the clasp. It snags sometimes."

"Let me help," Liam offered. She turned her back to him and he crouched down behind her to get a better look at the clasp in the dim red light. This close to her, he could smell the scent of her warm skin mixed with the soft fragrance of roses. It wasn't overpowering—more like strolling through a rose garden on a summer day. He inhaled it into his lungs and held it there for a moment. It was intoxicating.

He grasped the two sides of the clasp, ignoring the buzz of awareness that shot through his fingertips as he brushed her bare skin beneath it. With a couple of firm twists and pulls, it came apart. He gripped the zipper tab and pulled it down a few inches, revealing the back of the red satin panties she wore.

"Got it," he said with clenched teeth, standing back up and moving away before he did something stupid like touch her any more than was necessary. It was one thing to sit in the elevator in his underwear. It was another thing entirely to do it when he had a raging erection. That would be a little hard to disguise.

"Thank you," she said softly, her eyes warily watching him as she returned to her corner of the elevator.

As she started to shimmy the skirt down her hips, Liam turned away, although it took every ounce of power he had to do so. She was everything he liked in a woman. Feisty. Exotic. Voluptuous. And underneath it all, a caring soul. She wasn't one of those rich women that got involved in charity work because they had nothing better to do with their time. She really cared. And he appreciated that, even if it would cost him a few headaches in the future.

"Grazie, signore," she said with a sigh. "That does feel better."

Out of the corner of his eye, he saw her settle back down on the floor. "Is it safe?" he asked.

"As safe as it's going to get. Thank you for asking."

Liam looked over at her. She had tugged down her camisole to cover most everything to the tops of her thighs, although now a hint of her red bra was peeking out from the top. There was only so much fabric to go around, and with her luscious curves, keeping them all covered would be a challenge.

"You might as well just take those pants off now."

Liam chuckled and shook his head. Not after thinking about her satin-covered breasts. He didn't even have to touch her to make that an impossibility. "That's probably not the best idea at the moment."

Her brow wrinkled in confusion. "Why—" she started, then stopped. "Oh."

Liam closed his eyes and tried to wish his arousal away, but all that did was bring images of those silky red panties to his mind. "That's the challenge of being trapped in a small space with a beautiful, half-naked woman."

"You think I'm beautiful?" her hesitant voice came after a long moment of silence between them.

He planted his hands on his hips. "I do."

"I didn't expect that."

Liam turned to look at her. "Why on earth not? I think a man would have to be without a pulse to not find you desirable."

"I grew up in Beverly Hills," she said with a dismissive shrug. "I'm not saying I never dated in school—I did—but there was certainly a higher premium placed on the Malibu Barbie dolls."

"The what?"

"You know, the blond, beach-tanned girls with belly button piercings and figures like twelve-year-old boys? At least until they turn eighteen and get enough money to buy a nice pair of breasts."

"People in Hollywood are nuts," he said. "There was nothing remotely erotic about me as a twelve-year-old. You, on the other hand…" Liam shook his head, the thoughts of her soft curves pressing against the palms of his hands making his skin tingle with anticipation. He forced them into tight fists and willed the feeling away.

"It takes everything I've got not to touch you when I see you sitting there like that."

There was a long silence, and then her voice again. "Why don't you?"

Liam's jaw was flexed tight, and his whole body tensed as he tried to hold back the desire that was building inside for her. "I didn't think it was a good idea. I'm your boss. We have to work together. Things would get weird. Wouldn't they?"

Please let her say no. Please let her say no.

"I don't think so," she said, slowly climbing to her knees. "We're both adults. We know what this is and what it means." She crawled leisurely across the elevator floor, stopping in front of him. Her hands went to his belt buckle as she looked up at him through her thick, coal-black lashes. "What happens in the elevator, stays in the elevator, right?"

Liam didn't know what to say. He could barely form words as her hands undid his belt buckle, then the fly of his pants. But he didn't stop her. Oh, no. He wanted her too badly to let good sense interfere. Besides, they had time to kill, right? Who knew how long they'd be trapped in here.

His suit pants slid to the floor and he quickly kicked out of them and his shoes. Crouching down until they were at the same level, he reached for the hem of her camisole and pulled it up over her head. Francesca undid the clip holding her hair and the heavy, ebony stands fell down around her shoulders like a sheet of black silk.

The sight of her body in nothing but her red undergarments was like a punch to his guts. She was one of the sexiest women he'd ever seen—and she was mostly naked, and on her knees, in front of him.

How the hell had he gotten this lucky today?

Unable to hold back any longer, he leaned in to kiss her. They collided, their lips and bare skin slamming into one another. Francesca wrapped her arms around his neck and pulled her body against him. Her breasts pressed urgently against the hard wall of his chest. Her belly arched into the aching heat of his desire for her.

The contact was electric, the powerful sensations running through his nervous system like rockets, exploding at the base of his spine. He wanted to devour her, his tongue invading her mouth and demanding everything she could give him. She met his every thrust, running her own silken tongue along his and digging her nails frantically into his back.

Liam slipped his arm behind her back and slowly eased her down onto the floor. He quickly found his place between her thighs and dipped down to give attention to the breasts nearly spilling from her bra. It didn't take much to slip the straps from her shoulders and tug the bra down to her waist. The palms of his hands quickly moved in to take its place. He teased her nipples into firm peaks before capturing one in his mouth.

Francesca groaned and arched into him, her fingertips weaving into his thick, wavy brown hair. She tugged him back up to her mouth and kissed him again. There were no more thoughts of heat or sweat or broken elevators as he lost himself in the pleasurable exploration of her body.

And when he felt her fingers slide down his stomach, slip beneath the waistband of his underwear and wrap around the pulsating length of his erection, for a moment he almost forgot where he was, entirely.

Thank heavens for power outages.

* * *

Francesca wasn't quite sure what had come over her, but she was enjoying every minute of this naughty indulgence. Perhaps being trapped in this hot jail cell was playing with her brain, but she didn't care. There was just something about Liam. Sure, he was handsome and rich, but she'd seen her share of that kind of man in Washington, D.C. There was something about his intensity, the way he was handling the company and even how he handled her. She'd been fighting the attraction to him since she first laid eyes on him, and then his shirt came off to reveal a wide chest, chiseled abs and a sprinkle of chest hair, and she lost all her reasons to resist.

When he told her that she was beautiful, a part of her deep inside urged her to jump on the unexpected opportunity. To give in to the attraction, however inappropriate, and make a sexy memory out of this crazy afternoon.

She still wanted a solid, lasting relationship like her parents had. They'd been happily married for thirty years in a town where the typical wedding reception lasted longer than the vows. But having a fun fling in an elevator was in a totally different category. Liam would never be the serious kind of relationship, and she knew it, so it didn't hurt. This was a release. An amusing way to pass the time until the power was restored.

Francesca tightened her grip on Liam until he groaned her name into her ear.

"I want you so badly," he whispered. He moved his hand along the curve of her waist, gliding down to her hip, where he grasped her wrist and pulled her hand away. "You keep doing that and I won't have the chance to do everything I want to do to you."

A wicked idea crossed her mind. Francesca reached out with her other hand for the half-empty bottle of water beside them. "Let me cool you off then," she said, dumping the remains over the top of his head. The cool water soaked his hair and rushed down his face and neck to rain onto her bare skin. It was refreshing and playful, the cool water drawing goose bumps along her bare flesh.

"Man, that felt good," Liam said, running one hand through his wet hair as he propped himself up with the other. "I don't want to waste it, though." He dipped down to lick the droplets of water off her chest, flicking his tongue over her nipples again. He traveled down her stomach to where some of the water had pooled in her navel. He lapped it up with enthusiasm, making her squirm beneath him as her core tightened and throbbed in anticipation.

His fingertips sought out the satin edge of her panties and slipped beneath them. Sliding over her neatly cropped curls, one finger parted her most sensitive spot and stroked her gently. She couldn't contain the moan of pleasure he coaxed out of her. When he dipped farther to slip the finger deep inside her body, she almost came undone right then. The muscles tightened around him, the sensations of each stroke building a tidal wave that she couldn't hold back for much longer.

"Liam," she whispered, but he didn't stop. His fingers moved more frantically over her, delving inside and pushing her over the edge.

Francesca cried out, her moans of pleasure bouncing off the walls of the small elevator and doubling in volume and intensity. Her hips bucked against his hand, her whole body shuddering with the feeling running through her.

She had barely caught her breath when suddenly there was a jarring rattle. The silence was broken by the roar of engines and air units firing up, and the lights came back on in the elevator.

"You have got to be kidding me," he groaned.

And then, with Liam still between her thighs and their clothes scattered around the elevator, the car started moving downward. Francesca threw a quick glance to the screen on the wall. They were on the thirty-third floor and falling. "Oh, no," she said, pushing frantically at his chest until he eased back.

She climbed to her feet, tugging on her skirt and yanking her bra back into place. She didn't bother tucking in her camisole, but shrugged into her jacket. Liam followed suit, pulling on his pants and shirt. He shoved his tie into his pants pocket and threw his coat over his arm.

"You have my lipstick all over you," she said, noting less than ten floors to go. Liam ran his hand through his still wet hair and casually rubbed at his face, seeming to be less concerned than she was with how he looked when they walked out.

By the time the elevator came to the first floor and the doors opened, Francesca and Liam were both fully dressed. A bit sloppy, with misaligned buttons and rumpled jackets, but dressed.

They stepped out into the grand foyer where the building engineers and security guards were waiting for them. "Are you two—" one of the men started to speak, pausing when he saw their tousled condition "—okay?"

Liam looked at Francesca, and she could feel her cheeks lighting up crimson with embarrassment. He still had some of her Sizzling Hot Red lipstick on his face, but he didn't seem to care. "We're fine," he said. "Just hot, hungry and glad to finally be out of there. What happened?"

"I'm not sure, sir. The whole island lost power. Wouldn't you know it would be on such a hot day. Might've been everyone turning on their air conditioners for the first time today. Are you guys sure we can't get you anything? Three hours in there had to be miserable."

"I'm fine," Francesca insisted. The engineer's expression had been a wake-up call from the passionate haze she'd lost herself in. She'd very nearly slept with her boss. Her new boss. On his first day after they'd spent the morning fighting like cats and dogs. The heat must've made her delirious to have thought that was a good idea.

At least they'd been interrupted before it went too far. Now she just wanted to get a cab back to her hotel. Then she could change out of these clothes, shower and wash the scent of Liam off her skin. "Just have someone hail me a taxi to my hotel, would you?"

The engineer waved to one of the doormen. "Sure thing. It might take a minute because the traffic lights have been out and there's been gridlock for hours."

Without looking at Liam, Francesca started for the door, stepping outside to wait on the sidewalk for her car.

"Talk about bad timing," Liam said over her shoulder after following her outside.

"Fate has a funny way of keeping you from doing things you shouldn't do."

Liam came up beside her, but she wouldn't turn to look at him. She couldn't. She'd just get weak in the knees and her resolve to leave would soften.

"I'd like to think of it more as a brief interruption. To build some anticipation for later. Where are you headed?"

"To where I was going before my whole day got sidetracked—back to my hotel. To shower and get some work done. Alone," she added if that wasn't clear enough.

"Do you have plans for dinner tonight?"

"Yes, I do." She didn't. But going out to dinner with Liam would put her right back in the same tempting situation, although hopefully without power outages. She'd given in to temptation once and she'd been rescued from her bad decision. She wasn't about to do it again.

Liam watched her for a minute. Francesca could feel his eyes scrutinizing her, but she kept her gaze focused on the passing cars. "You said things wouldn't get weird. That we both knew what this was and what happened in the elevator stayed in the elevator."

Francesca finally turned to him. She tried not to look into the sapphire-blue eyes that were watching her or the damp curls of his hair that would remind her of what they'd nearly done. "That's right. And that's where it will stay. That's why I don't want to go to dinner with you. Or to drinks. Or back to your place to pick up where we left off. We've left the elevator behind us and the opportunity has come and gone. Appreciate the moment for what it was."

"What it was is unfinished," he insisted. "I'd like to change that."

"Not every project gets completed." Francesca watched a taxi pull up to the curb. It was empty, thank goodness.

"Come on, Francesca. Let me take you to dinner tonight. Even if just to say thank-you for the granola bar. As friends. I owe you, remember?"

Francesca didn't believe a word of that friend nonsense. They'd have a nice dinner with expensive wine someplace fancy and she'd be naked again before she knew it. As much as she liked Liam, she needed to stay objective where he was concerned. He was the new owner of ANS and she couldn't let her head get clouded with unproductive thoughts about him. They'd come to a truce, but they hadn't fully resolved their issues regarding her budget and the way forward for the network. She wouldn't put it past an attractive, charming guy like Liam to use whatever tools he had in his arsenal to get his way.

She stepped to the curb as the doorman opened the back door of the taxi for her.

"Wait," Liam called out, coming to her side again. "If you're going to leave me high and dry, you can at least tell me what you called me today in the board meeting."

Francesca smiled. If that didn't send him packing, nothing else would. "Okay, fine," she relented. She got into the cab and rolled down the window before Liam shut it. "I called you *figlio di un allevatore di maiali*. That means 'the son of a pig farmer.' It doesn't quite pack the same punch in English."

Liam frowned and stepped back from the window. The distance bothered her even though it was her own words that had driven him away. "I'd say it packs enough of a punch."

She ignored the slightly offended tone of his voice. He wasn't about to make her feel guilty. He'd deserved the title at the time. "Have a good evening, Mr. Crowe," she said before the cab pulled away and she disappeared into traffic.

Three

Liam had just stepped from his shower when he heard his cell phone ringing. The tune, "God Save the Queen," made him cringe. Had he told his great aunt Beatrice he was in Manhattan? She must've found out somehow.

He wrapped his towel around his waist and dashed into his bedroom where the phone was lying on the comforter. The words "Queen Bee" flashed on the screen with the photo of a tiara. His aunt Beatrice would not be amused if she knew what the rest of the family called her.

With a sigh, he picked up the phone and hit the answer key. "Hello?"

"Liam," his aunt replied with her haughty Upper East Side accent. "Are you all right? I was told you were trapped in an elevator all afternoon."

"I'm fine. Just hungry, but I'm about to—"

"Excellent," she interrupted. "Then you'll join me

for dinner. There's an important matter I need to discuss with you."

Liam bit back a groan. He hated eating at Aunt Beatrice's house. Mostly because of having to listen to her go on and on about the family and how irresponsible they all were. But even then, she liked them all more than Liam because they kissed her derrière. And that was smart. She was worth two billion dollars with no children of her own to inherit. Everyone was jockeying for their cut.

Everyone but Liam. He was polite and distant. He didn't need her money. Or at least he hadn't until the ANS deal came up and he didn't have enough liquid assets to buy a majority stake quickly. Other people also were interested in the company, including leeches like Ron Wheeler, who specialized in hacking businesses to bits for profit. To move fast, Liam had had to swallow his pride and ask his aunt to invest in the remaining shares of ANS that he couldn't afford. Together, they had controlling interest of the company, and by designating her voting powers to him, Aunt Beatrice had put Liam in charge.

Liam had every intention of slowly buying her out over time, but he wouldn't be able to do so for quite a while. So now, at long last, Aunt Beatrice had something to hold over his head. And when she snapped, for the first time in his life, he had to jump.

"Dinner is at six," she said, either oblivious or unconcerned about his unhappy silence on the end of the line.

"Yes, Aunt Beatrice. I'll see you at six."

After he hung up the phone, he eyed the clock and realized he didn't have long to get over to her Upper

East Side mansion in rush hour traffic. He'd do better to walk, so he needed to get out the door soon.

It was just as well that Francesca had turned down his dinner date so he didn't have to cancel. That would've pained him terribly, even after knowing what she'd called him.

"Son of a pig farmer," he muttered to himself as he got dressed.

He opted for a gray suit with a pale purple dress shirt and no tie. He hated ties and only wore them when absolutely necessary. Today, he'd felt like he needed to look important and in control at the board meeting. He didn't want the ANS directors to think they were in the hands of a laid-back dreamer. But as soon as he had a strong foothold in the company, the ties would be gone.

Tonight, he left it off simply because he knew to do so would aggravate Aunt Beatrice. She liked formal dress for dinner but had given up long ago on the family going to that much trouble. She did, however, still expect a jacket and tie for the men and a dress and hosiery for the ladies. It was only proper. Leaving off the tie would be a small but noted rebellion on his part. He didn't want her to think she had him completely under her thumb.

It wasn't until he rang the doorbell that he remembered her mentioning something about an important issue she wanted to discuss. He couldn't imagine what it could be, but he sincerely hoped it didn't involve him dating someone's daughter. Aunt Beatrice was single-minded in her pursuit of marriage and family for Liam. He couldn't fathom why she cared.

"Good evening, Mr. Crowe," her ancient butler Henry said as he opened the door.

Henry had worked for his aunt Liam's entire life and a good number of years before that. The man was in his seventies now but as spry and chipper as ever.

"Good evening, Henry. How is she tonight?" he asked, leaning in to the elderly man and lowering his voice.

"She's had a bee in her bonnet about something all afternoon, sir. She made quite a few calls once the power was restored."

Liam frowned. "Any idea what it's about?"

"I don't. But I would assume it involves you because you were the only one invited to dinner this evening."

That was odd. Usually Aunt Beatrice invited at least two family members to dinner. She enjoyed watching them try to one-up each other all night and get in her good favor. It really was a ridiculous exercise, but it was amazing what the family would do just because she asked. His grandfather, Aunt Beatrice's brother, had never had much to do with her, so neither did that branch of the family. It was only after all the others of the generation had died that she took over as matriarch. Then, even Liam's part of the family was drawn back into the fold.

Liam held his tongue as Henry led him through the parlor and into the formal dining room. When a larger group was expected, Aunt Beatrice would greet her guests in the parlor and then adjourn to the dining room when everyone had arrived. Apparently because it was just him they bypassed the formalities and went straight to dinner.

Aunt Beatrice was there in her seat at the head of the long, oak table, looking regal as always. Her gray hair was curled perfectly, her rose chiffon dress nicely accented by the pink sapphire necklace and earrings she paired with it. She didn't smile as he entered. Instead, she evaluated him from top to bottom, her lips tightening into a frown when she noted his lack of tie.

"Good evening, Aunt Beatrice," he said with a wide smile to counter her grimace. He came around the table and placed a kiss on her cheek before sitting down at the place setting to her right.

"Liam," she said, acknowledging him without any real warmth. That's why he'd always thought of her as royalty. Stiff, formal, proper. He couldn't imagine what she would have been like if she had married and had children. Children would require laughter and dirt—two things unthinkable in this household.

Henry poured them each a glass of wine and disappeared into the kitchen to retrieve their first course. Liam hated to see the old man wait on him. He should be in a recliner, watching television and enjoying his retirement, not serving meals to privileged people capable of doing it themselves. The man had never even married. He had no life of his own outside of this mansion.

"When are you going to let Henry retire?" he asked. "The poor man deserves some time off before he drops dead in your foyer."

Aunt Beatrice bristled at the suggestion. "He loves it here. He wouldn't think of leaving me. And besides, Henry would never die in the foyer. He knows how expensive that Oriental rug is."

Liam sighed and let the subject drop. Henry placed bowls of soup in front of them both and disappeared again. "So, what have you summoned me here to discuss tonight?" He might as well just get it over with.

There was no sense waiting for the chocolate soufflé or the cheese course.

"I received a phone call today from a man named Ron Wheeler."

Liam stiffened in his seat and stopped his spoon of soup in midair. Ron Wheeler was in the business of buying struggling companies and "streamlining" them. That usually involved laying off at least half the employees and hacking up the benefits packages of the ones who were left. Then he'd break the company up into smaller pieces and sell them off for more than the price of the whole. No one liked to hear the mention of his name. "And what did he have to say?"

"He heard I'd bought a large portion of Graham Boyle's ANS stock. He's made me an extremely generous offer to buy it."

At that, Liam dropped his spoon, sending splatters of butternut squash all across the pristine white tablecloth. Henry arrived in an instant to clean up the mess and bring him a new spoon, but Liam didn't want it. He couldn't stomach the idea of food at this point.

"Aunt Beatrice, your holding is larger than mine. If you sell him your stock, he'll gain majority control of the company. The whole network will be at risk."

She nodded, setting down her own spoon. "I realize that. And I know how important the company is to you. But I also want you to know how important this family is to me. I won't be around forever, Liam. This family needs someone strong and smart to run it. You don't need me to tell you that most of our relatives are idiots. My two sisters never had any sense and neither did their children. My father knew it, too, which is why he left most of the family money to me and your grandfather. He knew they'd all be broke and homeless without someone sensible in charge."

Liam didn't want to know where this conversation was going. It couldn't be good. "Why are you telling me this? What does it have to do with Ron Wheeler?"

"Because I think you're the right person to lead the family after I'm gone."

"Don't talk like that," he insisted. They both knew she was too mean to die. "You have plenty of years ahead of you."

Her sharp blue gaze focused on him, an unexpected hint of emotion flashing in them for a fleeting second before she waved away his statement. "Everyone dies, Liam. It's better to be prepared for the eventuality. I want you to take my place and be family patriarch. As such, you would inherit everything of mine and serve as executor of the family trusts."

The blood drained from Liam's face. He didn't want that kind of responsibility. Two billion dollars and a family full of greedy suck-ups chasing him around? "I don't want your money, Aunt Beatrice. You know that."

"Exactly. But I know what you do want. You want ANS. And as long as I have my shares, you won't truly have it. I could sell at any time to Ron Wheeler or anyone else who gives me a good offer."

Liam took a big swallow of wine to calm his nerves. Aunt Beatrice had never held anything over him. She couldn't because until now he hadn't needed her or her money and she knew it. But he'd made a critical error. He never should've agreed to this stock arrangement with her. He'd given her the leverage to twist him any way she wanted to. "Why would you do that? I told you

I would buy that stock from you at what you paid or the going rate, if it goes higher."

"Because I want you to settle down. I can't have you leading this family while you play newsman and chase skirts around D.C. I want you married. Stable. Ready to lead the Crowe family."

"I'm only twenty-eight."

"The perfect age. Your father married when he was twenty-eight, as did your grandfather. You're out of school, well established. You'll be a prize to whatever lucky woman you choose."

"Aunt Beatrice, I'm not ready to——"

"You will marry within the year," she said, her serious tone like a royal decree he didn't dare contradict. "On your one-year wedding anniversary, as a gift I will give you my shares of ANS stock and name you my sole beneficiary. Then you can truly breathe easy knowing your network is secure, and I can know this family will be cared for when I'm gone."

She couldn't be serious. "You can't force me to marry."

"You're right. You're a grown man and you make your own decisions. So the choice is entirely yours. Either you marry and get the company you want and more money than most people dream of…or you don't and I sell my shares to Ron Wheeler. Tough choice, I understand." At that, she returned to her soup as though they'd been discussing the weather.

Liam didn't know what to say. He wasn't used to anyone else calling the shots in his life. But he'd given himself a vulnerability she had been waiting to exploit. She'd probably planned this from the very moment he'd come to her about buying ANS. Liam leaned his head into his hand and closed his eyes.

"If you don't know any suitable ladies, I can make a few recommendations."

He was sure she'd just love that, too. Thankfully she'd stopped short of deciding who he should marry. "I think I can handle that part, thank you. I've been seeing someone," he said quickly, hoping she didn't ask for more details about the fictional woman.

Aunt Beatrice shrugged off the bitter tone in his voice. "Then it's time the two of you got more serious. Just remember, you have a year from today to marry. But if I were you, I wouldn't dawdle. The sooner you get married, the sooner ANS will be yours."

Francesca had deliberately avoided Liam since they'd returned to D.C., but she couldn't put off speaking to him any longer. She needed to know if they were going to be sponsoring the Youth in Crisis gala or not. It was a week and a half away. It was already too late to pull out, really, but if he was going to insist they couldn't do it, she needed to know now.

She waved as she passed his assistant's desk. "Afternoon, Jessica."

The woman looked up at her with a wary expression. "You don't want to go in there."

Francesca frowned. Did she mean her specifically, or anyone? Liam couldn't still be mad about the whole elevator thing. Could he? "Why?"

"He's been in a foul mood since we left New York. I'm not sure what happened. Something with his family, I think."

"Is everyone okay?"

Jessica nodded her head. "He hasn't had me send flowers to anyone, so I would assume so. But he's not taking calls. He's been sitting at his desk all morning flipping through his address book and muttering to himself."

Interesting. "Well, I hate to do it, but I have to speak with him."

"As you wish." Jessica pressed the intercom button that linked to Liam's phone. "Mr. Crowe, Ms. Orr is here to see you."

"Not now," his voice barked over the line. Then, after a brief pause, he said, "Never mind. Send her in."

Jessica shrugged. "I don't know what that's all about, but go on in."

Francesca gripped the handle to his office door and took a deep breath before going inside. She'd dressed in her most impressive power suit today and felt confident she would leave his office with what she wanted. The emerald-green pantsuit was striking and well-tailored. Her black hair was twisted up into a bun, and she had a silk scarf tied around her neck. Not only did she feel good in the outfit, she felt well-covered. Liam had already seen too much of her body. She intended to keep every inch out of his sight from now on.

As she opened the door, she saw Liam sitting at his desk just as Jessica had described. He was flipping through an address book, making notes on his desk blotter. As she came in he looked up and then slammed the book shut.

"Good morning, Ms. Orr." His voice was a great deal more formal and polite than it was the last time they'd spoken. Of course, then they'd been recently naked together.

"Mr. Crowe. I wanted to speak to you about the Youth in Crisis gala. We don't have much time to—"

"Have a seat, Francesca."

She stopped short, surprised at his interruption. Unsure of what else to do, she moved to take a seat in the guest chair across from his desk. Before she could sit, he leaped up and pointed to the less formal sitting area on the other side of his office.

"Over here, please. I don't like talking to people across the desk. It feels weird."

Francesca corrected her course to sit in the plush gray leather chair he'd indicated. She watched him warily as he went to the small refrigerator built into the cabinets beside his desk.

"Would you like something to drink?"

"I don't drink at work."

Liam turned to her with a frown and a bottle of root beer in his hand. "At all? I have bottled water, root beer—my personal favorite—and some lemon-lime soda. I don't drink at work, either, despite the fact that if anyone wanted to be in a drunken stupor right now, it would be me." He pulled a bottle of water out of the fridge and handed it to her. "To replace the one we... *used up* in the elevator."

Francesca started to reach for the bottle, then froze at the memory of water pouring over his head and onto her own bare chest. Damn, he'd said that on purpose to throw her off her game. Pulling herself together, she took the bottle and set it on the coffee table unopened.

Liam joined her, sitting on the nearby sofa with his bottle of root beer. "I have a proposition for you."

She didn't like the sound of that. "I told you that I wasn't interested in dinner."

Liam watched her intently with his jewel-blue eyes as he sipped his drink. "I'm not asking you to dinner. I'm asking you to marry me."

Francesca was glad she hadn't opted to drink that water or she would've spit it across the room. She sat bolt upright in her seat and glared at him. "Marry you? Are you crazy?"

"Shhh…" he said, placing his drink on the table. "I don't want anyone to hear our discussion. This is very important. And I'm dead serious. I want you to be my fiancée. At least for a few months."

"Why me? What is going on?"

Liam sighed. "I've put myself in a vulnerable position with the company. I couldn't afford all of Graham Boyle's stock, so my aunt owns the largest share of ANS, not me. She's threatening to sell it to Ron Wheeler if I don't get married within a year."

Ron Wheeler. That was a name that could send chunks of ice running through her veins. Charity didn't help the bottom line in his eyes. Francesca, her staff and the entire department would be out the door before the ink was dry on the sale. And they would just be the first, not the last to go if he were in charge. "Why would she do that?"

"She wants me married and settled down. She wants me to be the strong family patriarch when she's gone and doesn't believe my playboy ways are appropriate. I think she's bluffing, really. I'm hoping that if I get engaged, that will be enough to soothe her. In the meantime, I'm going to work with my accountant and financial advisor to see if I can arrange for a line of credit large enough to buy her out. I have no expectation that we'll actually have to get married."

"I should hope not," she snapped. Francesca had some very strong ideas about what a good marriage was made of and blackmail was not the ideal start. "Don't you have anyone else you can ask? You've known me less than a week."

Liam looked over to the book on his desk and shook his head. "I've gone through every woman's name in my address book and there's not a single suitable candidate. All those women would look at this as a romantic opportunity, not a business arrangement. That's why you're my ideal choice."

A business arrangement? That's just what a girl wanted to hear. "So if this is just a business arrangement, that means you have no intention of trying to get me into bed, right?"

Liam leaned closer to her and a wicked grin spread across his face. "I didn't say *that,* but really, that's not my first priority here. I'm asking you for several reasons. First, I like you. Spending time with you shouldn't be a hardship. My aunt will expect the relationship to appear authentic and she'll sniff out the truth if she thinks we're faking it. After our time in the elevator, I think you and I have enough chemistry to make it realistic. And second, I know I can count on you because you want something from me."

Francesca opened her mouth to argue with him and then stopped. She knew exactly where this was going. Tit for tat. "The Youth in Crisis gala?"

He nodded. "If Ron Wheeler gets a hold of this company, everything you've worked for will be destroyed. The only thing I can do to protect this company and its employees is to get engaged as soon as I can. For your assistance, I'm offering the full financial support of ANS for the Youth in Crisis charity ball. I'll even pledge to top the highest private donation with my own money. I look at it as an investment in the future of the network. And all you have to do is wear a beautiful diamond ring and tolerate my company until my aunt backs down."

It felt like a deal with the devil and there had to be a catch. "You said it had to appear authentic. Define *authentic*."

Liam sat back in his seat and crossed his leg over his knee. "No one is going to follow us into the bedroom, Francesca, and I won't make you do anything that you don't want to do. But everything we can do to convince people we are a couple in love would be helpful."

She shook her head and looked down at her lap. This was all so sudden. The idea of being Liam's fiancée, even if just temporarily, wasn't so bad. She'd be lying to herself if she said she hadn't thought about their time in the elevator as she lay alone in bed each night. But his fiancée? Publicly? What would she tell her family? She couldn't tell them the truth. And her friends? She would have to lie to everyone she knew.

But the alternative was unthinkable. She cared too much about ANS and its employees to let the company fall into Ron Wheeler's hands. Going along with Liam's plan would protect the company and earn her the charity gala she wanted so badly. When the arrangement was no longer necessary, her friends and family would just have to believe that things had soured between them and they broke it off. She could live with that. It wasn't as though they were actually going to get married.

She looked up in time to see Liam slide off the couch to his knees and crawl across the floor until he was kneeling at her feet. He looked so handsome in his navy suit, his dark, beautiful blue eyes gazing into her own. He took her hands into his, his thumb gently stroking her skin. With him touching her like that, she'd probably agree to anything.

"Francesca Orr," he said with a bright, charming smile. "I know I'm just the humble son of a pig farmer, but would you do me the honor of being my temporary fiancée?"

Four

Liam watched Francesca's terrified expression, waiting for her answer. He could see the battle raging in her head. He understood. He was having to make sacrifices for the company and what he wanted, too. He felt guilty for dragging her into his mess, but she really was the perfect choice. If she could walk away from that elevator like nothing happened, she could do the same with this engagement. In the end, they could go their separate ways, both having gotten what they wanted.

Her dark brown eyes focused on him for a moment, then strayed off to his shoulder. Her expression of worry softened then, her jaw dropping with surprise.

Confused, Liam turned to look at his shoulder. Perched there on the navy fabric was a lone ladybug. He'd opened the window of his office this morning when he was suffocating from the pressure and needed some fresh air. The tiny insect must've been a stowaway.

Francesca untangled her hands from his and reached out to scoop the ladybug from his shoulder. She got up from her seat and walked over to the window. Opening it wide, she held her palm out to the sun and watched the bug fly out into the garden outside the network offices.

She stood looking out the window for several minutes. Liam was still on his knees, wondering what the hell had just happened, when he heard her speak.

"Yes, I will be your temporary fiancée."

He leaped to his feet and closed the gap between them in three long strides. "Really?"

She turned to him, her face calm and resolute. She looked really beautiful in that moment. Serene. The dark green of her suit looked almost jewel-like against the tan of her skin. It made him want to reach out and remove the pins from her hair until it fell loose around her shoulders. He liked it better that way.

"Yes," she said. "It's the right answer for everyone."

Liam was elated by her response yet confused about what had changed. There had been a moment when he had been absolutely certain she was going to tell him no. He'd already been mentally putting together a contingency plan. He was going to offer her obscene amounts of cash. And if that didn't work, he was going to find out if Jessica, his secretary, was married. "What helped you decide?"

"The ladybug. They're an omen of good luck. Having one land on you means you are a blessed soul. It was a sign that I should accept your proposal."

Liam knew better than to question her superstitions as long as they ruled in his favor. "Well, remind me to thank the next ladybug I come across."

Francesca chuckled. "I think you owe the entomology department at Georgetown a nice check."

"And I will get right on that. After I take my fiancée to lunch and let her pick out her engagement ring."

Her head snapped up to look at him. "So soon?"

"Yes," he insisted. "The sooner my aunt hears about this, the better. That means ring shopping, an announcement in the paper here and in New York and public sightings of the happy new couple. I intend to update my relationship status on Facebook before the day is out."

Her eyes widened with every item on his list. She wasn't sold on this arrangement, ladybug or no. "Before it hits the papers, I need to make a few calls. I don't want my family to find out from someone else. This is going to come out of the blue."

Liam nodded. That was understandable. He had a few calls of his own to make. First, to his mother and younger sister, both living in Manhattan.

His family was miserable at keeping in touch, but this was big enough news to reach out to them. They had always been like ships passing in the night, waving to one another as they went along their merry way. His parents were very outgoing and traveled quite a bit his whole life. But that changed after his father died three years ago when his car hit black ice on the highway coming home from a late business meeting. Since then, his mother had kept to her place in Manhattan, nearly becoming a recluse. He just assumed she was bad about calling until she stopped altogether—then he knew something was really wrong. His sister had moved in with her to keep an eye on the situation, but it hadn't helped much.

When he spoke with them, it was because he was

the one to reach out. Maybe the news of the engagement would be exciting for her. He felt bad lying to his mother about something like that, but if it got her up and out of the apartment, he didn't care.

Liam had often wondered, even more so in the past week, how things would be different if his father hadn't been in that accident. Where would everyone be now? Perhaps Aunt Beatrice would've wanted to hand the family to him instead, and Liam wouldn't be in this mess.

That was a pointless fantasy, but it reminded him of his next call. Once he was done with his mother, he had to inform Aunt Beatrice of the "happy" news. He didn't have many people to tell, but he could see by the expression on Francesca's face that she had the opposite problem. She must have a large, close family. An out-of-the-blue engagement would send up a hue and cry of mass proportions.

"I know this is a big deal. And not at all what you were expecting when you walked in here today. But it's all going to work out." He moved closer to her and put his arms gently around her waist. She reluctantly eased into his embrace, placing her hands on his lapels and looking up into his eyes. "I promise."

The dark eyes watching him were not so certain. He needed to reassure her. To make her feel more at ease with their new situation and prove they were compatible enough to pull this off. He only knew of one way to comfort a woman. He slowly lowered his lips to hers, giving her time to pull away if she needed to. She didn't. She met his lips with her own, her body leaning into his.

The kiss wasn't like the one in the elevator. They had come together then in a passionate and desperate rush. Two people in a stressful situation looking for any way to deal with their nervous tension. This kiss was soft, gentle and reassuring. They were feeling their way around each other. Her lips were silky against his, the taste of her like cinnamon and coffee. She made a soft sound of pleasure that sent a warm heat running through his veins. It reminded him of the cries she'd made beneath him that first day. It beckoned him to explore further, but he didn't dare push this moment too far. At this point, she could change her mind and no one would know the difference.

He couldn't risk running her off. They both needed this fake engagement to work. And if it did, he would eventually have his chance to touch her again. The thought gave him the strength to pull away.

Francesca rocked back onto her heels, her cheeks flushed and her eyes a little misty. She took a deep breath to collect herself and took a full step back from him. "Well," she said with a nervous laugh, "that authenticity thing shouldn't be an issue."

Liam smiled. "Not at all. Are you hungry?"

She straightened her suit coat and shrugged. "A little."

"Okay. You're not starving, so let's go ring shopping first. Then if we run into anyone at lunch, we'll have it and can share the news like a happy couple would."

"I need to get my purse from my office before we leave. I'll meet you at…" Her voice trailed off.

"The elevator?" he said with a grin.

She blushed. "Yes, I'll meet you at the elevator."

They strolled out of Pampillonia Fine Jewelry two hours later and, frankly, Francesca was exhausted. Who knew jewelry shopping could be so tiring? She almost wished that Liam had just popped the question with ring in hand like most men would and saved her the trouble of choosing.

Instead, they had spent the past couple of hours quibbling. She was worried that Liam was spending too much, especially considering it was a fake engagement. Liam insisted that Francesca needed to choose a ring large enough for people to see from a distance. Fake or not, the engagement needed to be splashy so people like his aunt would take notice.

They finally came to a compromise when she got tired of arguing and just let herself choose the ring she'd want if this were a real relationship and she had to wear the ring every day for the rest of her life. By the time they left, she was certain there was no doubt in the jeweler's mind that they were a real couple getting a head start on a lifetime of fussing at one another.

When it was all over, Francesca was the proud owner of a two-carat emerald-cut diamond solitaire framed with micro-pavé set diamonds in a platinum split band with diamond scrollwork. It was a stunning ring, and as they walked to the restaurant where they had lunch reservations, she almost couldn't believe it was on her hand. The weight of it pulling on her finger kept prompting her to lift her hand to look at it.

Francesca had dreamed her whole life of the day a man would give her a ring like this. The ring was right. But everything else was so wrong. Her life had taken a truly surreal turn since she had woken up this morning.

"Are you hungry now?" he asked as they approached the bistro with outdoor seating. It was perfect for an early May lunch; luckily, the Manhattan heat wave had not affected the D.C. area. It was pleasant and sunny in the high seventies with a breeze.

She still wasn't really hungry. Her stomach hadn't come to terms with the day's events. But she needed to eat or her blood sugar would get low and she'd spend the afternoon eating cookies out of the network vending machines. "I could eat. I think."

They followed the hostess, who took them to a shaded table for two on the patio. As nice as it was outside, she'd secretly hoped to get a table indoors. The street was so busy with foot traffic that she was certain to see someone she knew. Of course, she could just as easily run into someone inside. Between her and Liam, they knew a lot of people in this town. Francesca wasn't sure she was ready to play the gushing new fiancée for them yet.

Liam pulled her chair out for her and saw that she was comfortably seated before taking his own seat.

"I'm starving," he said, picking up the menu.

Francesca had to admit she wasn't surprised. Liam seemed to be constantly hungry when she was around him. "No breakfast?"

He shook his head. "I really haven't eaten much since I had dinner at my aunt's house. Killed my appetite, you know?"

"I do," she agreed. Nothing on the menu looked appealing, so she settled on a spinach salad with chicken. At the very least she was eating something figure-friendly.

She had a wedding dress to fit into, after all.

The thought crept into her brain, startling her upright in her seat. Where had that come from?

"Are you okay?" Liam asked.

"Yes," she said dismissively. "I just remembered something I need to do when we get back to the office."

Liam nodded and looked back at the menu. Francesca shook her head and closed her eyes. There would be no wedding and no wedding dress. It didn't matter how real their kisses seemed or how quickly her whole body responded to Liam's touch. It didn't matter that she had a luxury condo's worth of diamonds on her hand. Because she wasn't really engaged. She was Liam's fake fiancée. It was a business arrangement, nothing more, despite what she had to tell her friends and family.

The waiter took their orders and left with their menus. Feeling awkward, Francesca sipped her water and eyeballed her ring. She didn't know what to say to her new fiancé.

"Now that all the engagement stuff is arranged, I wanted to talk to you about something else, too."

She looked up at him with a sense of dread pooling in her stomach. She couldn't take any more surprises today. "No, Liam, I will not have your baby to make your aunt happy."

He laughed, shaking his head. "No babies, I promise. This is strictly work-related. I've been kicking around this idea for a few days, but the nonsense with my aunt sidetracked me. I wanted to ask…you're friends with Ariella Winthrop, aren't you?"

Francesca sighed. Her friend Ariella had been the media equivalent of the Holy Grail since the inaugural ball in January where it was revealed that the successful events planner was the newly elected president's long-lost daughter. How many journalists and garden-variety busybodies had asked Francesca about her friend since the scandal hit? More than she could count. Yes, they were friends. They had been for several years. That didn't mean she had anything useful to share with the press, even if she would tell—and she wouldn't. Ariella was adopted. She hadn't even known who her birth father was for sure until the DNA test results came back a little more than a month ago.

"I am," she said, her tone cautious.

"I was wondering if you could talk to her for me. I've got an idea that I think she might be interested in, but I wanted to run it by you first. I know ANS reporters and old management were responsible for the whole mess with President Morrow and her. I was hoping we could make a sort of goodwill gesture to them both."

"A fruit basket?" she suggested.

"A televised reunion show with Ariella and the president."

Francesca groaned aloud. That was a horrible idea. "Go with the fruit basket. Really."

Liam held up his hand. "Hear me out. I know lots of rumors and misinformation are swirling around on the other networks, especially because everyone involved isn't talking to the press. ANS obviously has stayed out of the story after everything that happened. I want to offer them the opportunity to publically set the record straight. Give them a chance to meet and clear the air without any spin or dramatic angles."

"That has 'exploitive' written all over it."

"And that is why I would give you total control over the show. You're her friend and she trusts you. You could work directly with the White House press secretary and see to it that no one is even remotely uncomfortable. No other network will offer them an opportunity like this, I guarantee it."

Francesca couldn't hold back her frown. She didn't like the sound of this at all. If it went badly and ANS ended up with mud on its face, there would be no coming back from it and Ariella might never forgive her. "I don't know, Liam."

"This is a win-win for everyone involved. Ariella and the president get to tell their story, their way. ANS will get the exclusive on their interview and it will help us make amends for the hacking scandal. It can't go wrong. You'll see to it that it doesn't turn into a circus. It's perfect."

Perfect for ratings. But Francesca wasn't so sure television was the right environment for her friend to be reunited with her famous birth father. That was an important moment for them both. A private moment. Ariella hadn't spoken much to her about the situation, but Francesca knew it was hard for her friend.

"Just promise me you'll ask her. If she doesn't want to do it, I'll let the whole idea drop."

The waiter came with their lunches, placing them on the table and briefly interrupting their conversation.

"I'll talk to her," Francesca agreed after he left. "But I can't promise anything. She made one short statement to the press, but aside from that, she's turned down every interview request she's received."

"That's all I ask. Thank you."

Francesca speared a piece of chicken and spinach with her fork. "At last, the dirty truth comes out. You're just marrying me for my political connections."

"A completely unfounded accusation," he said with a wicked grin. "I'm marrying you for that slammin' body."

Francesca met his gaze, expecting to see the light of humor there, but instead she found a heat of appreciation for what he saw. It was the same way he'd looked at her in that elevator when she'd had only a camisole to cover her. Today, she was deliberately covered head to toe, but it didn't matter. Liam apparently had an excellent memory.

A warmth washed over her, making her squirm uncomfortably in her seat with her own memories of that day. She had wanted him so badly in that moment, and if she was honest with herself, she still did. Things were just so complicated. Would giving into her desire for him be better or worse now that they were "engaged"?

She wished she hadn't opted for the silk scarf around her neck. It was strangling her now. Her left hand flew to her throat and started nervously tugging at the fabric. "I…well, I uh…"

A voice called to them from the sidewalk, interrupting her incoherent response. "Francesca, what is that I see on your hand?"

So much for not running into anyone she knew. On the other side of the wrought-iron railing that separated the bistro seating from the sidewalk was her friend Scarlet Anders. The willowy redhead owned a party planning company with Ariella that specialized in weddings and receptions. She could smell a new diamond from a mile away.

"Scarlet!" she said, pasting a smile on her face and hoping Scarlet didn't see through it. "How are you feeling?" she asked to distract her from the ring. Her friend had suffered a head injury earlier in the year and had temporarily lost her memory. It was a reasonable question that might buy Francesca a few minutes to get their engagement story straight.

Scarlet wrinkled her nose. "I'm fine, really. The doctors say there's not a single, lingering side effect from my accident. Now stop fussing over me, you staller, and let me see that hand."

Reluctantly, Francesca held out her left hand, letting the flawless diamond sparkle in the sunlight. Scarlet looked at the ring, then at Liam and back at her. "You are engaged to Liam Crowe. *Liam Crowe.* You know, when Daniel proposed to me, I told you and Ariella almost the moment it happened."

That was true, Francesca thought guiltily. And under any other circumstances, she would've done the same thing. This just didn't feel like a real engagement. Because it wasn't. "It just happened," she insisted, grinning widely with feigned excitement at her groom to be. "We just picked out the ring before lunch."

Scarlet smiled. "It's beautiful. You two are so sneaky. I didn't even know you guys were dating. How did this happen?"

"We, uh…" Francesca realized she had no clue what to say. They hadn't really gotten around to deciding what they're relationship history was. Certainly the truth wouldn't do, or people would think they were crazy. "Actually, um…"

"We started seeing each other a while back when I first started looking to buy ANS," Liam interjected. "With everything going on, we wanted to keep it quiet for a while. But after being trapped in that elevator with Francesca, I knew I had to spend the rest of my life with her."

Francesca swallowed her snort of contempt as Scarlet sighed with romantic glee. "That is so sweet. I can't believe you didn't tell *me,* of all people, but you two are just adorable together. So when is your engagement party? You have to let Ariella and I do it for you."

"No," Francesca insisted. "You've been so busy with Cara and Max's wedding and now, planning your own big day." The former newscaster and the public relations specialist for the White House press secretary had married at the end of March. Scarlet's beau, Daniel, had proposed to her at the wedding reception. "Don't worry about us. We're probably not going to—"

"Nonsense," Scarlet said. "I insist. I'm on my way back to the office right now. I'll tell Ariella the good news and we'll get right to work on it. When would you like to have it?"

"Soon," Liam interjected, cutting off another of Francesca's protests. "This weekend, if at all possible. We can't wait to share our excitement with all our friends and family."

Scarlet's eyes widened, but she quickly recovered with a pert nod. She was used to dealing with the unreasonable demands of powerful D.C. couples. "I'm sure we can make that happen. Short notice makes it harder to find a venue, but I've got a couple of people who owe me some favors. For you, I'm thinking an afternoon garden party. Something outdoors. Light nibbles, champagne punch. Maybe a gelato bar. How does that sound?"

Francesca choked down a sip of her water. "That sounds beautiful." And it did. It was just what she would've chosen for her engagement party. Her friend knew her well. She just wished they weren't wasting their efforts on an engagement that wouldn't lead to a loving marriage.

Scarlet was bursting with excitement. Francesca could see the lists being made in her head. Flowers, caterers, maybe even a string quartet to serenade the guests. Scarlet did everything with a stylish flair that was famous in elite D.C. society. "I will give you a call tomorrow and work out some details."

"Just tell me where to send the check." Liam smiled.

"Absolutely," Scarlet said. "Talk to you soon." She swung her bag over her shoulder and disappeared down the sidewalk with an excited pep in her step. She really did live for this stuff.

Francesca wished she could work up as much enthusiasm. And she needed to if they were going to pull this off. Because this was really happening. Really, *really* happening.

What on earth had she done?

Five

Liam hadn't planned on their having dinner that night, but seeing Francesca with Scarlet had made it absolutely necessary. They really knew nothing about each other. They had no relationship backstory. Once the news of their engagement got out, people would start asking questions and they needed to get their stories straight.

Usually this kind of discussion happened before the engagement, but they were working on a steep learning curve, here. After the waiter took their orders, Liam settled back into his seat and looked at his fiancée. He knew she was beautiful, feisty, caring and exciting. He knew that he desired her more than any other woman he'd ever known. And yet, he knew almost nothing about who she was and where she'd come from. That was a problem.

"So, Francesca, tell me all about yourself. I need to know everything to play this part properly and convince everyone we're really together."

"I feel like I'm trying to get a green card or something." She took a sip of wine as she tried to determine where best to start. "I grew up in Beverly Hills. My father is a Hollywood movie producer, as you know. He met my mother on a film set in Sicily and they eloped within a month of meeting."

"So they have no room to complain about our quick engagement?"

"Not at all." She smiled. "Although that didn't stop my father from giving me an earful on the phone this afternoon. I had to assure him that we would have an extended engagement to keep him from hopping a jet over here and having a chat with you."

"The longest engagement in history," Liam quipped.

"My parents are my model for what a marriage should be. It's what I've always hoped to have one day when I get married."

Liam took note. Francesca wanted the real deal for herself, just like her parents. This was probably not what she thought her engagement would be like. He felt bad about that. But she still had her chance to have the fairy tale with the next guy. This was just a temporary arrangement.

"I have a younger sister, Thérése," she continued, "who lives in San Francisco. She's a fashion photographer. I moved to D.C. after graduation to go to Georgetown."

"I went to Georgetown, too. Maybe we were there at the same time." Francesca recited the years and, thankfully, they partially overlapped with his own. He'd graduated two years before she had. "That's excellent," he said. "I think if we tell people that we dated back in college and then met up again this year, it will make the speed of this relationship more palatable. What did you study?"

"I got a degree in communications with a minor in political science. I'd originally intended to become a political news commentator."

"It's a shame you didn't. I would've loved to have you on my big screen every night. It's funny we didn't meet until now. I had a minor in communications. I'm surprised we didn't have a class together."

Francesca shrugged. "Maybe we did. A lot of those classes were pretty large."

Liam shook his head. There was no way he could've been in the same room with Francesca and not have seen her. Even in one of those freshman courses they held in the huge auditoriums. His cocky, frat boy self would've picked up on those curves and asked her out in a heart-beat. "I would've noticed you. I'm certain of that."

Francesca blushed and started fidgeting with the gold pendant around her neck that looked like some kind of horn. For dinner, she'd changed into a burgundy wrap dress with a low V-cut neckline and an abundance of cleavage. He'd noticed the necklace earlier, but every time he thought to ask about it, he'd been mentally side-tracked by the sight of her breasts.

"So what's that necklace about? You seem to have it on whenever I've seen you."

She looked down at it before holding it out a little for him to see it better. "It's a *corno portafortuna*. My *nonna* gave it to me. It's Italian tradition to wear one to ward off the evil eye. You never know when some-one might curse you, especially in this town. I wear it for good luck."

The way the horn rested right in the valley of her

breasts was certainly lucky for him. It gave him an excuse to look at the firm globes of flesh he could still feel in his hands and pretend he was admiring her jewelry. "In the elevator you mentioned spending summers in Italy with your grandmother."

"Yes, I spent every summer in Sicily from when I was about five until I graduated from high school. My mother would travel with me when I was younger, but once I reached junior high, I got to fly alone. My mother said it was important for me to keep in touch with my culture. My *nonna* would teach me authentic Italian recipes and tell me stories about our family. My sister and I both learned a good bit of Italian over the years. I don't remember as much as I should now."

"You know all the dirty words," Liam noted.

"Of course." She laughed. "You always remember the words and phrases that you shouldn't know."

"You picked up all your superstitions there too?"

"Yes. Italians are a very superstitious people. My *nonna* told me she only taught me a few of them. It's amazing. My mother never really cared for all that, but it was something special I shared with *Nonna*. She died last year, but the superstitions keep her alive in my mind."

"Thank goodness she told you the one about ladybugs or I might be in big trouble right now. Any bad luck omens I should keep an eye out for?"

"Hmm…" Francesca said thoughtfully. "There are the ones most people know about—broken mirrors and such. Never leave your hat on the bed. Never set a loaf of bread upside down on the table. Birds or feathers in the home are bad luck. If you spill salt, you have to toss some over your shoulder. The most unlucky number is seventeen. Never marry on a Friday. There are a million of these."

"Wow," Liam said. "I'm probably doomed. I've been running around for years, cursed, and never knew it."

Francesca smiled, easing back in her seat to let the waiter place their food on the table. "I think you've done pretty well for yourself without it."

That was true. He'd taken the seed money from his father and built quite a name for himself in broadcast media. He was only twenty-eight. Who knew what else he could accomplish with most of his career still ahead of him? Closing the deal with his aunt and taking full control of ANS could be the launching pad to bigger, better things. Especially if the two-billion-dollar inheritance came through.

His brain couldn't even comprehend having that much money. He tried not to even think about it. He could only focus on one thing at a time and right now, it was pulling off this engagement and buying ANS outright. He'd put his financial manager on the task before he even sat down to look for a bride. Hopefully, it would all work out. But even his worries were hard to concentrate on with such a beautiful woman sitting across the table from him.

"How about some more random trivia about you? Likes and dislikes," Liam said.

"My favorite color is red. I adore dark chocolate. I'm allergic to cats. I can cook, but I don't. I hate carrots and yellow squash. My middle name is Irish and impossible to spell or pronounce properly."

Liam had to ask. "Wait, what is it?"

"My middle name? It's pronounced *kwee-vuh,* which is Gaelic for *beautiful.* Unfortunately, in English it's pronounced absolutely nothing like it's written. *C-A-O-I-M-H-E*." She spelled out the name for him and then said it again. "Try explaining that to the woman at the DMV."

Liam laughed, not trusting himself to repeat the name without slaughtering it. "My middle name is Douglas. Not very exciting or hard to spell."

"I envy you."

"What about your dad's side of the family? You haven't mentioned much about them."

"My dad isn't that close with his family, which is silly considering they live in Malibu, only about thirty miles from Beverly Hills. I only ever saw my grandparents on holidays and birthdays. I'm much closer with my mother's side of the family."

"Sounds more like my family. I almost never see them. Tell me something else about you."

"What else? I never exercise—I hate to sweat. And I enjoy luxurious bubble baths and long walks on the beach." She finished with a laugh. "This is turning into a lame personal ad."

"It's not lame. If I ran across it, I'd be messaging your in-box in an instant."

"Thanks. But enough about me. What about you?" Francesca asked. "Your turn to tell me all about Liam Crowe."

Dinner had been very nice. The conversation flowed easily and Francesca had to admit she had a good time. She enjoyed spending time with Liam. Honestly, she liked him. He was handsome, smart, funny and easy to talk to. It was nice to hear him talk about his family and his work. He was so passionate about his career; it made her understand just how important the success of ANS was to him. A part of her wished she had met him in college. Who knows what would've happened then?

Well, that wasn't true. She knew what would've happened. They would've dated, she would've fallen for him and he would've broken it off at some point, breaking her heart. Liam wasn't much of a long-term guy. They were only engaged now because his aunt had recognized that in him and twisted his arm.

Despite that, he seemed to be taking the whole thing pretty well. She wasn't exactly sure how Liam felt about their forced proximity, but he didn't let it show if he wanted to be someplace else. Actually, he'd been quite complimentary of her, listening to her when she spoke and watching her over his wineglass with appreciative eyes.

Liam pulled up his gray Lexus convertible outside her town house and killed the engine. He turned in his seat to face her, a shy smile curling his lips. He watched her collect her purse and sweater, not speaking but also not making a move to let her out of the car, either.

Their plotting dinner suddenly felt like a date and it made her a little nervous. It was silly considering he'd not only seen her naked, but they were engaged. Technically.

"I had a good time tonight," she said, feeling stupid the moment the words left her lips.

"Me, too. I, uh, wanted to say thank-you again for doing this for me. And, you know, for the company. I feel like I've hijacked your entire life today."

Francesca tried to think about what she was supposed to have done today. She certainly had plans of some kind, but Liam had wiped her memory clean along with her calendar. "I'm sure I didn't have anything important planned and if I did, it will still be around for me to do tomorrow."

"Do you have time on your schedule to have some engagement portraits taken? I wanted a picture to put with the newspaper announcement."

"I think so. Just have Jessica look at my calendar in the morning. Do I need to wear anything in particular or do something special with my hair or makeup?"

Liam watched her, shaking his head. "You're perfect just as you are. I couldn't ask for a more beautiful fiancée."

Francesca blushed. She couldn't help it. To hear him talk, she was the most beautiful woman in the world. It was ridiculous. She was a pretty enough woman but nothing special. He had a knack for making her feel special, though. "You're just sucking up so I don't change my mind."

"Absolutely," he admitted. "But it's easy when it's true. You don't know how much I've thought about you since that afternoon we spent together. And now, spending all day with you, I've been struggling with myself. I've spent the past three hours trying not to kiss you. I'm not sure I can hold out much longer."

Francesca couldn't help the soft gasp of surprise when he spoke so honestly about his desire for her. Before she could think of something intelligent to say, he leaned across her seat and brought his lips to hers.

It wasn't their first kiss. Or even their second, but somehow it felt like it. It lacked the raw heat of their time in the elevator and the reassuring comfort of this morning's kiss. This one felt like the kiss of a blossoming romance. His hand went to the nape of her neck, pulling her closer to him and gently massaging her with his fingertips.

His mouth was demanding but not greedy, coaxing her to open to him and give in to the pleasure he promised. She felt herself being swept up in his touch. It was so easy, just like letting herself flow with the current of a river. It felt natural to let her tongue glide along his, to let her fingers roam through the thick strands of his wavy hair.

His lips left hers, traveling along the line of her jaw to nibble the side of her neck. The sensation of it sent a wave of desire through her whole body. When his hand cupped her breast through the thin microfiber of her dress, she leaned into his touch, moaning softly in his ear.

It wasn't until her eyes peeked open and she saw the giant diamond on her hand that she came to her senses. This relationship was supposed to be for show. One that appeared authentic to friends and family. But as Liam had said, no one would follow them into the bedroom. Somehow, Francesca knew that if she crossed that line, it would be hard for her to keep this relationship in perspective.

Liam was her fiancé, but he would never be her husband. He wasn't in love with her, nor was she in love with him. Sex would just blur the lines.

Francesca gently pushed at Liam's shoulders. He pulled away, watching her with eyes hooded with desire. His breath was ragged. That was one hell of a kiss. And it was begging for one hell of a night together. She could tell that he intended to come inside. A nice dinner, a bottle of wine, good conversation, a dynamic kiss… now she was supposed to invite him in for coffee and take off her dress. That was all too much too soon, no matter how badly she might want him.

Francesca reached for the door handle. "Good night, Liam."

"Wait," he said with a frown as he reached out to her. "Good night?"

She nodded, clutching her purse to her chest as a sub-par barrier between them. "It's been a long day filled with a lot of excitement. You went from my boss to my fiancé just a few short hours ago. I think adding 'lover' to the list tonight is a bad idea."

Liam sighed but didn't try to argue with her. Instead, he opened his car door and came around to help her out. He escorted her to her doorstep.

Francesca paused, clutching her keys in her hand. Right or wrong, she couldn't help leaning into him and placing a quick but firm kiss on his lips.

"I'll see you tomorrow at the office."

"Yes, I'm engaged." Liam sat back in his office chair and looked at the newly framed photograph of Francesca and himself that sat on the corner of his desk. They'd had it taken for the newspaper announcement, and Liam couldn't help sending a copy to the Queen Bee herself. When the phone rang the next afternoon, he wasn't surprised.

"Congratulations to you both. I didn't expect you to move so quickly on my offer," she noted, her tone pointed. She obviously thought that Liam was trying to pull one over on her somehow. She missed nothing. "I did give you a year, not a week, to get engaged."

"Well," Liam began, "I told you I had been seeing someone. You helped me realize that I needed to move forward in my relationship. Francesca and I are perfect for each other—I was just hesitant to take that last step. Thank you for the encouragement." He hoped he'd managed to work out the bitterness from his voice after practicing this speech several times before her call.

"That is wonderful, Liam. The picture of the two of you is lovely. I've sent Henry to have it framed for the mantle. She's quite the striking young lady. Where did you meet her?"

She was fishing for details. Thank goodness they'd worked all this out at dinner. "We met the first time in college through mutual friends and dated for a while." He recalled their fabricated past, linking it together with what he'd told Scarlet at lunch. "When I started looking into buying ANS, we ran into each other at a media event. She works there doing community outreach programs and we started seeing each other again."

Liam had no doubt that his aunt was taking notes and would have someone look into the fact that they had both attended Georgetown at the same time. "What a lovely coincidence that you two would find each other again. It must be meant to be."

"I think so."

"I hope both of you will be very happy together. I can't wait to meet her. In fact, I'm coming to D.C. later this month to speak to Congress. I'd love for the three of us to have dinner and celebrate while I'm there."

Liam frowned at the phone, glad for the miles between them and the lagging technology of camera phones that prevented her from seeing his pinched expression. He'd never known his aunt to have any political involvement before beyond writing checks. If she was coming to D.C., it was to check on him. She didn't trust

Liam a bit and rightfully so. They would have to perfect their lovey-dovey act before she arrived. Frankly, Francesca had been miserable at it when they ran into Scarlet.

It wasn't just the details of their relationship that had tripped her up. Her smile of engaged bliss had looked a little pained. She'd lacked the excited glow. She had had to be asked to show the engagement ring, whereas any other woman would thrust it out at anyone that would look.

Despite her hesitation to embark on a physical relationship the other night after dinner, something had to be done. She needed some real romantic inspiration to draw on because she couldn't fake it. Liam was all too happy to provide it.

He may have told Francesca that he didn't choose her with the intention of seducing her, and that was true. If they did become lovers, it would simply be a pleasant bonus to a potentially unpleasant scenario.

Heaven knew, he wanted Francesca. Every time he closed his eyes he saw her in the elevator. Red panties. Flushed cheeks. Soft, passionate cries of pleasure echoing in the small space. Yes, he didn't need a romantic entanglement complicating this arrangement, but he'd be lying if he said he didn't want to pick up where they'd left off.

Sex wouldn't be a problem as long as they both knew that's all it was. Given the way Francesca had writhed beneath him and walked away like nothing happened, she knew how to play that game. He just had to coax her into taking another spin at the wheel.

Gripping the phone, Liam struggled to remember what his aunt had just said. The mere thought of Francesca's red panties had completely derailed his train of thought. *Dinner.* Aunt Beatrice was coming to town and wanted to have dinner. "Absolutely," he said. "Francesca is very excited to meet you."

"I'm sure she is. I hope you two have a lovely engagement party tonight. I'm going to let you go. I need to call Ron Wheeler and let him know I'm turning down his proposal. For now," she added, making it clear they weren't out of the woods quite yet.

"It was good to speak with you," he said between gritted teeth. "I'll see you soon."

Hanging up the phone, he spun in his chair to look back at the photo of Francesca and him. His aunt made him absolutely crazy, but if this scheme landed that voluptuous, feminine form back in his arms, he just might have to send the Queen Bee a thank-you card.

Six

Francesca was fastening on her last earring when the doorbell rang. Giving herself one final look in the mirror, she was pretty pleased with how her outfit turned out. She'd purchased something new for the engagement party—a pale turquoise dress that was strapless and hit just below the knee. Around the waist was a cream-colored sash with a fuchsia flower for a pop of color. It came with a crocheted cream shrug to keep her shoulders warm when the sun went down.

She'd opted to wear her hair half up, with the front pulled back into a stylish bump and the rest loose in long waves down her back. Wearing her hair back highlighted her face and the sparkling aquamarine jewelry she was wearing at her ears and throat. And, of course, she was wearing the most important piece of her ensemble—her engagement ring.

Satisfied, she went down the stairs to the front door.

She watched Liam waiting patiently through the peep-hole. He was looking very handsome in a light gray suit, ivory dress shirt and turquoise tie to coordinate with her outfit.

Even though he'd dropped her off the other night after dinner, he hadn't been inside her town house yet. They'd decided he should pick her up and get familiar with her home just in case someone asked questions.

So far, no one had, and it was likely no one would. None of their friends in D.C. were remotely suspicious about their quick engagement. Romance seemed to be in the air this spring. So many of her friends had gotten married or engaged, so they were on trend. It was only Liam's crafty aunt they had to please.

"Hello," she said as she opened the door and gestured for him to come inside. "Come on in. This is my place."

"Very nice," he said, strolling into the living room and admiring his surroundings.

Francesca had always liked her home. She'd bought the small, red-brick town house near the university while she was a student. It was only two bedrooms, but the floor plan was open and the walled courtyard off the living room was the perfect oasis from the world. When she'd first bought it, nearly every room in it was white. She'd painted each room a warm, inviting color and filled them with lush fabrics and comfortable fixtures. That was her biggest update over the years. She loved her place.

She led him into the two-story living room so he could see out into her little garden and to the nicely remodeled kitchen she rarely used. "It's not very big, but it suits me. I love the location—right across from the park."

"You've done a lot with the place," he said. "It looks comfortably lived in. Very much what I'd expect for you. My town house still looks like a showroom model. I never got around to hiring a decorator. Who did yours?"

"I did," Francesca said, her nose wrinkling. "I couldn't let someone else decorate my house. That's too personal."

Liam shrugged. "You've got the eye for it. Maybe while we're engaged, I'll let you decorate mine."

She turned away from him without answering and went in search of her clutch instead. She didn't like the sound of that at all. It wasn't as though she would be moving into his house one day. She didn't need to put her own personal stamp on his space or leave anything behind of her once all this was over. That made things seem more permanent than they were. But she wasn't going to make much of it. They had a long night to get through without her adding more worries to the pile.

"Are you ready?" she asked.

"Absolutely."

Liam followed her out and then escorted her to the curb, where his convertible was waiting for them. Once he merged into traffic, they didn't have far to go. Scarlet and Ariella had secured a location at one of the large historical mansions in Georgetown. The two-hundred-year-old estate had acres of gardens with fountains and an overabundance of spring flowers this time of year. It was the perfect location for a sunny, happy engagement party.

As they pulled onto the property, the valet opened the doors, pointed them to the garden entrance and took the car around back to park it with the others.

Standing on the lawn, facing her engagement celebration, Francesca was more nervous than she cared to admit. Her knees were nearly shaking. She'd done okay enduring the excited hugs and fielding questions from her friends and coworkers, one by one. But this was almost everyone she knew at one time. It made her wonder if she could pull this off. An engagement party. *Her* engagement party.

Liam sensed her hesitation and approached her. Putting his hands on the back of her upper arms, he stroked her gently, reassuringly. "Everything will be fine. You look beautiful. I'm sure Scarlet and Ariella did a great job with all the arrangements. There's no need to be nervous."

"I know," she said with a shake of her head. She looked down toward the grass, but Liam's finger caught her chin and turned her face up to him.

"You can do this. I know it. But I have to say you are missing something."

Her eyes widened in panic. What had she forgotten? Ring? Check. Lipstick? Check. Overwhelming sense of paranoia? Check. "What did I forget?"

"You don't have the rosy blush of a young woman in love. But I do believe I can fix that." Liam leaned in and pressed his lips to hers.

As much as she had tried to deny her attraction to Liam, her body always gave her away. The heat of his touch immediately moved through her veins and she could feel the tingling of the kiss from the top of her head to the tips of her toes. She suddenly felt flush under her dainty sweater. Her knees were still shaking, although for different reasons than before. She gripped at his lapels to keep steady and pull him closer to her.

Liam's kisses were dangerous. She should've learned

that the very first day. A girl could get lost in one if she wasn't careful. And right now, it seemed like the perfect escape from everything else. Couldn't they just stay in each other's arms here on the front lawn? That seemed like the kind of thing a new couple might do, right?

When Liam finally pulled away, he held her close to keep her from swaying. She felt a definite heat in her cheeks as she looked up at him. "No lipstick on you this time," she noted.

"I was being more cautious today. But it worked—you officially have the bridal glow. Let's get in there before it wears off."

He looped her arm through his and escorted her down the stone pathway that led into the garden reception.

At first the party was a blur. There were easily a hundred and fifty people there, which was impressive on such short notice. Someone announced their arrival, and a rush of people came over to hug and congratulate them. There were pictures and toasts to the happy new couple. Francesca worried it would be hard to keep up the act, but after a little practice and a little champagne, showing people her ring and gushing about how beautiful the party was became easier and easier.

It wasn't long before Francesca was able to slip away from Liam and the crowds to get herself a drink and admire her friends' party-planning handiwork. Scarlet and Ariella really did an excellent job. The garden itself was beautiful, but she could spot the touches they'd added, like white paper lanterns in the trees and a gauzy fabric and flower arch behind the string quartet. The layout of the food and seating areas generated the perfect traffic pattern through the space. It was those details that made what her friends did special. Hassle-free events were their forte.

She picked up a glass and filled it at the four-foot-high silver punch fountain. Just as the lifted the frothy pink drink to her lips, she heard a woman's voice from behind her.

"That's got champagne in it, you know."

Francesca turned to find Ariella with a silver tray of pastel petit fours in her hands. "Am I not allowed to have champagne at my own engagement party?"

Her friend smiled and passed the tray off to one of the catering staff. "That depends on why you and Liam Crowe are in such a rush to get married."

"I am not pregnant," Francesca said with a pout. She should've known that rumor would be one of the first to start circulating. They liked nothing better than juicy gossip in these circles and they weren't above making some up if it was in short supply. She swallowed the whole glass of punch just to prove the rumor wrong.

"Good." Ariella refilled Francesca's glass and filled one of her own, then gestured over to a few chairs under a wisteria tree dripping with purple flowers. "So, just between you and me, what's going on?" she asked once they were seated.

Francesca knew her friend would grill her, although not in the same way that Aunt Beatrice probably would. She just wanted the details so she could understand and be happy for her. Or concerned, depending on if she thought she was being stupid or hasty. That's what good girlfriends did. They kept your head on straight. "It all happened so quickly, I can hardly tell you. The moment I saw him, it was like the last few years we've been apart never happened. There were fireworks." That wasn't exactly a lie. It was more like armed missiles, but there were explosions nonetheless.

Ariella looked into her eyes, searching her face for a moment. Then, satisfied, she smiled and patted Francesca on the knee. "Then I'm happy for you. I just wish you had told us what was going on."

Francesca wished she could really tell her what was going on. She could use a sounding board, but Liam had been adamant that no one know about their arrangement. No one. That was tough for her, considering how close she was with her friends and family.

"Everyone has been so busy with their own lives. I just decided to keep things quiet until there was something to tell."

"How'd your dad take the news?" Ariella asked.

"Ah." She sighed, "you know Dad. He'll adjust eventually. He's concerned that we're rushing things, and that he had no idea who my groom even was. I had to remind him that he and my mother met and eloped within a month. He didn't want to hear that."

Ariella smiled. "I imagine not."

Hoping to shift the subject, Francesca decided to use the topic of fathers to fulfill her first obligation to Liam. "Can I talk to you about something?"

"Sure," Ariella said. "Anything."

Francesca nodded. "Okay. Now I want you to tell me 'no' the moment you're uncomfortable with the idea, but I told Liam I would ask. Now is as good a time as any."

"He wants an interview?" she said wearily. Francesca could tell the last few months were really wearing on her friend.

"Not exactly. He wants to offer you and President Morrow the opportunity to meet and get your story out there. A televised reunion show. No spin, no intruding interview questions. Just you and your father, however you want to do it. Liam has even said he'd put me in charge of the show to make sure you'd be comfortable with it. I told him that I thought it was—"

"Okay."

Francesca's head shot up and she stared at Ariella. Surely she'd heard that wrong. "What?"

She shrugged. "I said okay. If the president is okay with doing the show, I think it's a great idea. We've gone too long without saying anything publicly, and I think it's starting to hurt both of us in the court of public opinion. Neither of us has done anything wrong, but the silence makes us look like we have something to hide."

"But do you think television is the right place for you to be reunited with your birth father? Won't that be hard for you?"

"Not any harder than anything else that's happened this year. Frankly, I'd be relieved to clear the air so the news networks can find some other story to sniff out. Tell Liam I'm in."

Francesca took another large sip of her champagne punch and sighed. Everyone had lost their minds—she was certain of it. "Okay, great," she said, feigning enthusiasm. "I'll let Liam know."

Liam had to admit that it was an excellent engagement party. One of the better ones he'd been forced to attend over the years. He was exhausted and well-fed, as he should be. If and when he did get married, he intended to keep D.C. Affairs Event Planners in his address book.

It was dusk now. The party was winding down, with

guests making their way out amid glowing paper lanterns and white twinkle lights.

He'd lost track of Francesca a little while earlier as he started talking politics with a few other men. Now, he picked up his champagne glass and went in search of his elusive fiancée. That sounded so odd to say, even just in his head.

He found her sitting alone at a table near one of the cherub fountains.

"Hey, there," he said as he approached. "Thought you'd run off on me."

Francesca smiled wearily and slipped off one of her heels. "I'm not running anywhere right now."

"Are you ready to go?"

"Yes. I think the party is over. And was successful, I might add. I got several people to agree to buying tickets to the Youth in Crisis gala next week."

"You're not supposed to recruit at our engagement party."

She shrugged. "Why not? It's what I do, just like you talk politics all the time with folks." She slipped her shoe back on and stood gingerly. *"Ahi, i miei piedi."*

Liam watched her hobble a few steps and decided the walk to the car would be too far for her. "Stop," he insisted, coming alongside her and sweeping her up into his arms.

"Oh!" she hollered in surprise, causing a few people left at the party to turn and look their way. They immediately smiled at his romantic gesture and waved good-night to them.

Francesca clung to his neck, but not with a death grip. "You didn't have to do this," she said as he walked the path to the front of the house.

"I don't have to do a lot of things, but I do them because I want to. Gray Lexus convertible," he said to the valet, who immediately disappeared to the car lot.

"I think I can manage from here."

"What if I'm doing this for selfish reasons? What if I just like holding you this way?" he asked. And he did. He liked the way she clung to him. The way her rose perfume tickled his nose and reminded him of their time together in the elevator. His body tightened in response to the press of her breasts against his chest and the silk of her bare legs in his arms. He didn't want to put her down until he could lay her on a plush mattress and make love to her the way he'd wanted to for days.

Francesca's only response was a sharp intake of breath as she turned to look into his eyes. She watched his face with intensity, reading his body's reactions through his expression. He saw an acknowledgment in her eyes—something that told him she was feeling the same way. She opened her mouth to say something when the car pulled up beside them.

Liam wanted to know what she was about to say, but instead, she turned away and struggled in his arms. He reluctantly set her down in the grass and went around to his side of the car and got in. The moment had passed and whatever she had to say was left unspoken.

It wasn't until the car pulled up outside her town house that they spoke again. And when they did, it was all at once in a jumble of words.

"Would you like to come in?"

"I had a great time today."

"So did I."

"Yes."

Francesca smiled at the way they'd talked over each

other. "Now that we have that all cleared up, come in and I'll make us some coffee."

Liam was thrilled to get an invitation inside tonight. He got out and opened her door, following her up the brick stairs to her entranceway. He laid a gentle hand at the small of her back as she unlocked the dead bolt and he felt her shiver beneath it, despite the warm evening. She couldn't help responding to his touch, he noted. If he had anything to say about it, they wouldn't worry too much about coffee until the morning.

They went inside and he followed her to the kitchen, where she dropped her purse on the counter and slipped out of her heels. "So much better," she said with a smile. "Now, coffee." Francesca turned to the cabinets and started pulling out what she needed to brew a pot.

While she scooped beans into the machine, Liam slipped off his coat, draped it on one of the bar stools and came up behind her. He wrapped his arms around her waist and pressed the full length of his body against her. He swept her hair over one shoulder and placed a warm kiss on the bare skin of her neck.

The metallic coffee scoop dropped to the counter with a clank as Francesca reached out to brace herself with both hands. "You don't want coffee?" she asked, her voice breathy as his mouth continued to move across her skin. She pressed into him, molding her body against his.

Liam slipped her sweater down her shoulders. "Coffee would keep me awake. I think I'd like to go to bed." He pushed the firm heat of his arousal against her back and let his hands roam over the soft fabric of her dress. "What about you?" he asked. He knew Francesca had been in a war between her body and her mind since they met. She'd practically run from him the other night, yet when he kissed her, he could tell she wanted more.

But tonight, this step had to be her decision. Playing the happy couple would be much easier the next few weeks if he wasn't battling an erection whenever they were together. Sex wasn't required in their arrangement, but damn, being engaged was a really great excuse to indulge.

"No," she said.

Her words caused Liam's hands to freeze in place. *Had she just said no?* Damn. He must've been reading her wrong. Did she really only invite him in for coffee? Maybe she was a better actress than he thought.

Before he could pull away, Francesca turned in his arms to face him and wrapped her arms around his neck. She looked up at him with her large dark eyes, a sly smirk curling her pink lips. "I don't want to go to bed," she explained. "I want you right here."

Liam was all too happy to grant her wish. With a slide of his arm, he knocked her bag to the floor and cleared the countertop bar. He encircled her waist with his hands and lifted her up to sit at the rounded edge of the granite slab. His hands slid up the smooth length of her legs, pushing the hem of her turquoise dress high enough to spread her thighs and allow him to settle between them.

"How's this?" he asked, gripping her rear end and tugging her tight to him.

Francesca smiled and wrapped her legs around his waist. *"Perfetto."*

She leaned in to kiss him, and the floodgates opened. The moment their lips met, everything they'd held back for the past week came rushing forward. Their hands moved frantically over each other, pulling at zippers and buttons until they uncovered skin. Their tongues glided along one another, tasting, tempting and drinking it all in.

Liam couldn't get enough of her. The feel of her skin, the soft groans against his mouth as he touched her. He tried to be gentle as he unzipped her dress and pushed the hem up to her waist, but his patience was coming to its end. Especially when Francesca pulled the dress up over her head and he caught a glimpse of the hot pink lace panties and strapless bra she was wearing.

He took a step back to appreciate the view of her body and give himself a moment to recover. As badly as he wanted her, he wasn't going to rush this. Francesca delicately arched her back, reaching behind her to unfasten the bra and toss it aside. The sight of her full, round breasts was his undoing. His palms ached to cover them.

"Touch me," Francesca whispered, noting his hesitation. "I want you to."

"Are you sure? The other night…"

"That was then. Now I'm ready and I don't want to wait any longer."

He was ready too, but first things first. With his eyes focused on hers, he slipped off his unknotted tie and shrugged out of his shirt. The belt, pants and everything else followed until the only stitch of clothing on the two of them were those pink panties. Stepping back between her thighs, he put a condom on the counter and let his hands glide up her outer thighs to her lace-covered hip. "Are these your favorite pair?" he asked.

Francesca shook her head. He was glad. He was at the point of not caring if they were. He'd order ten pair to replace them tomorrow. His fingers grasped the fabric and gave it a hard tug. There was a loud rip, and the panties gave way as scraps in his hands.

At last. Her beautiful nude body was on full display in front of him. This time there was no power restoration to interrupt them, no reason for them to hold back.

Liam placed one forearm across the small of her back and used the other to press down on her chest until she was lying across the breakfast bar. He leaned over her and his lips joined both hands as they made their way over her breasts and down her stomach. His mouth left a searing trail down her belly, pausing at her hip bone as one hand sought out the moist heat between her thighs.

Francesca gasped and squirmed against him. Her back arched off the counter, her hands clawing futilely at the cold stone beneath her. She was ready for him, and as much as he wanted to take his time, he had to have her now. They had all night to savor one another.

Slipping on the condom, Liam gripped her hips and entered her in one, quick movement. Sinking into her hot, welcoming body was a pleasure he'd rarely experienced before. A bolt of sensation, like lightning, shot down his spine and exploded down his arms and legs, making his fingertips tingle where he touched her. He gritted his teeth, balancing on the edge of control as he eased out, then buried deep inside her again.

Francesca pushed herself up, wrapping her legs around his waist and her arms around his neck. Pressing her bare breasts against his chest, she whispered, "Take me," into his ear, flicking the lobe with her tongue.

Gripping at her back and pulling her so close to the edge she might fall without his hold, he did as he was told. He filled her again and again, losing himself in her until she cried out with pleasure and his legs began to shake. It was only then that he let go. Moving quickly, he gave in to the sensation of her body wrapped around his own and flowed into her with a deep growl of long-awaited satisfaction.

Seven

Francesca rolled over and snuggled into her blanket, opening her eyes only when a weight kept the covers from moving the way she wanted. The sunlight was streaming in through her bedroom window, illuminating the wide, bare back of Liam beside her.

What had she done?

She'd had a night of fantastic, passionate sex with her fake fiancé—that's what she'd done. Giving up on the blanket, she moved slowly onto her back, hoping not to wake him. She wasn't quite ready to face the morning after with the man she wasn't going to marry.

She glanced under the sheet at her nude body and cursed that she didn't think to slip into *something* once it was over. Bringing her hand up to her head, she swallowed a groan. This situation was complicated enough. Feigning an engagement wasn't for the faint of heart. Had she really added sex to the mix? On her kitchen counter, of all places? It was a good thing she didn't cook.

Now things were going to go from complicated to downright tricky. Liam was her boss. Her pretend fiancé. She had no business sleeping with either, much less both. And yet she was undeniably attracted to him. She couldn't help it.

He was handsome, wealthy, powerful.... He had a wicked sense of humor and a boyish smile that made her heart melt a little when he looked at her. And most important, he cared about his employees. They'd gotten off on the wrong foot over the budget, but that issue aside, she respected him for what he was doing. She respected him even more for the lengths he was willing to go to protect the network.

Liam was just the kind of man she could fall for—and hard. The only problem was that he wasn't the kind of man that would feel the same about her.

Francesca took relationships seriously. She wasn't one for flings, despite losing her sense in the elevator, and she certainly didn't make a habit of sleeping with men when she didn't see any relationship potential.

She wanted a marriage like her parents had. Victor and Donatella Orr had been married thirty years. When she was growing up, they'd set a good example of what a relationship should be. They argued, but they compromised and never held grudges. They were affectionate and understanding. They allowed each other their space, yet were always certain to spend quality time together as a family and as a couple.

At twenty-seven, Francesca had yet to run across a man she could have that kind of relationship with. Some were too clingy; others were too self-absorbed. Some were quick-tempered or arrogant. Then there were the kind like Liam—work-focused dreamers who looked at marriage as something they'd do later. They indulged in a variety of women, never taking anything but their jobs seriously. They were the kind of men who would wake up at fifty and realize they had missed out on their chance for a family unless they could find a willing younger woman with a fondness for expensive gifts.

Despite being engaged to Liam, he was the last man on Earth she would marry. And that's why she knew sleeping with him was a mistake. As a passionate woman, she put her heart in everything she did. But she couldn't put her heart into this. She couldn't look at her engagement ring and their portrait together and imagine it was anything more than a well-crafted fantasy.

Francesca turned to look at Liam as he grumbled in his sleep and rolled onto his back. The blankets fell across his torso, his hard, muscular chest exposed to the early-morning sunlight. She wanted to run her fingertip along the ridges of his muscles and bury her hands in the patch of dark hair across his chest. She wanted to reach under the covers and wake him up in the most pleasant way possible.

This sure didn't feel like a business arrangement.

Turning away, she spied her robe hanging on the knob of her closet door. Easing silently out of bed, she snatched the silk wrap off the handle and slid into it. She gave another glance to Liam, still sleeping, and slipped out of the room.

Downstairs, she found she could breathe a little easier. At least until she saw the scraps of her pink underwear on the kitchen floor. She snatched them off the tile and dumped them in the trash, and then went around gathering other bits of their clothing. She tossed the pile onto her sofa and went to the front door to pick up the paper. Laying it onto the kitchen table, she decided to make coffee. The caffeine would help her think so she could sort all this out.

The last few drops were falling into the pot when she heard Liam's shuffling footsteps across her hardwood floors. A moment later, he appeared in the kitchen wearing nothing but the suit pants she'd just gathered up.

"Morning," she said, pouring a cup for both of them.

"You snuck out on me," Liam complained, his voice still a touch low and rough with sleep. He ran his fingers through his messy hair and frowned at her with displeasure.

"I promised you coffee last night," she explained. "I had to come down here and make it so it was ready when you woke up." That sounded much better than saying she'd gotten weirded out and had to leave. "How do you take it?"

"One cream, one sugar," he said, sitting at the small round table in her breakfast nook. He unfolded the paper and started scanning the articles, oblivious to the nerves that had driven her to the kitchen.

Francesca busied herself making their coffee and grabbed a box of pastries from the counter. She set the two mugs and the carton on the table and plucked two napkins from the container in the center of the table. "Breakfast is served."

"Thank you," he said, looking up from the paper. "Our party made the society pages in the Sunday edition." Liam slid the section with their photo across the table to her. "I should clip it out and send it to the Queen Bee."

"I'm sure she hated missing it. My friends throw parties even she couldn't find fault with. Oh—" Francesca said, pausing to take a sip of her hot drink. That had reminded her of the important information she hadn't shared with Liam yet. "I forgot to tell you that Ariella said yes."

Liam looked up from the paper. "Ariella said yes to what?"

"I got a chance to talk to her at the party about the televised reunion show. I can't fathom why, but she's agreed to do it if the president is willing."

Liam's eyes grew wide, and he folded the paper back up as he grinned. "That's excellent. Wow. How could you forget to tell me something like that? We've been together since the party."

Francesca looked at him over her cup with an arched eyebrow. "Yes. We were together *all* night. And highly occupied, if you recall."

Liam grinned. "Indeed, we were. It's just as well because there was nothing I could do about it last night." He picked a pastry out of the box and set it on his napkin, sucking some icing from his thumb. "Well, now you'll need to contact the White House press secretary to see if President Morrow will participate."

"Me?"

"Yes. I told you that you would be in charge of the event. That means the ball is in your court."

"The Youth in Crisis gala is Saturday night. I've got my hands full with that."

"I have every confidence," he said with a meaningful gaze, "that you can handle everything I'm giving you and more. It's likely the ball won't really get rolling on the show until after the gala, and you just need to get White House buy-in. By the time everything is in place, the show will probably air in June."

Francesca could handle June. "I'll call over there Monday morning," she agreed. Part of her hoped the president and his staff would see what a bad idea this was. She knew it would mean good ratings, and maybe a boost in public opinion for ANS, but it felt wrong. If she had been adopted, she didn't think she'd want those first reunion moments captured for the world to see.

"Sounds great." Liam set aside the folded paper and reached his hand across the table to rest on hers. "Thank you for asking her. I know you felt uncomfortable about it."

"It's Ariella's decision to make, not mine. If she thinks it's the right choice, far be it for me to tell her no. It's her life."

"I think you'll do a great job running the show. I know it isn't something you've handled at the network before, but you'll do a bang-up job. Everything has been so crazy since I started at ANS, but I really believe that we can bring this network back. If all goes well, I'll get absolute control of the stock and we can end the fake engagement. The exclusive with the president and his daughter will earn us Brownie points and market share for our time slot. I know I can rebuild this network—with your help. So thank you for everything you've done so far."

"Don't thank me yet," she said, fidgeting with her coffee mug. A lot of pieces had to click together for these miracle scenarios to work out. And deep in her heart, Francesca worried that eventually, things would start to go awry.

* * *

Monday morning, Francesca breezed into Liam's office without Jessica's usual announcement. He looked up from his computer as she entered and a wide grin broke out across his face. He *should* be smiling after the weekend they'd spent together. "I see you're enjoying the new privileges of being the owner's bride-to-be."

"Exclusive access, anytime," she said with a grin.

Liam was glad to see her relaxed and happy. At first, he wasn't sure they could pull this off. Liam would never admit to that out loud; this had to work or he'd lose the network. And he knew Francesca had her own worries. She wore every emotion on her face. But after their time together this weekend, he was certain they both had sunnier outlooks on the arrangement. The lines of doubt were no longer wrinkling her brow, replaced with a contented smile that suited her much better.

Francesca set a to-go cup of coffee and a bag of Italian breakfast cookies in front of him. She was going to get him addicted to those things and he'd never be able to find them without her help.

"Grande drip with one cream, one sugar," she announced.

"Just how I like it," he said, turning in his chair to give her a hello kiss.

Francesca leaned into him but pulled away before his hands roamed too far. As much as it annoyed him to not be able to touch her when and where he wanted, he understood. Their relationship might be for the sake of the company, but public displays of affection at the office were a little much. She sat down in the guest chair with her own cup.

"Have you called the White House yet?" he asked.

"It's nine in the morning and I just handed you a hot, fresh coffee from the bakery. No. I haven't been to my office yet."

"Okay, sorry," he said, taking a sip. "You know I'm excited to move this plan forward."

"I know. I'll call once I get to my desk. Hopefully it won't take very long. I have a million things to wrap up this week before the gala on Saturday."

Liam nodded, but the details of the event didn't really interest him. The gala was really just a blip on his radar. And they were only doing it because she had agreed to be his fiancée. He couldn't have justified the expense given the state of the network. As it was, every mention of centerpieces and orchestras made dollar signs run through his mind.

"Now about the gala," she continued. "I've got most everything in place. Ticket sales have gone well and our sponsorship will see to it that it's the best year we've had yet. You'll need to make sure your tuxedo goes to the cleaners."

Liam made a note on his blotter so he wouldn't forget to ask Jessica about that later. "Check."

"And write a speech."

"What's that?" Liam looked up, his brow furrowed. He didn't like public speaking. As a matter of fact, he hated it. Avoided it at all costs and had since prep school debate class. Not even his aunt's declaration of mandatory matrimony made his stomach turn the way approaching a crowd of people with a microphone could do. There was a reason he preferred to be behind the camera instead of in front of it.

"As the major event sponsor, it's your job to give the

evening's welcome speech and encourage everyone to donate well and often."

"I don't remember Graham ever doing that." He tried to remember the times he'd gone. Maybe Graham did speak, but Liam was far too interested in his date for the evening to pay much attention. "Shouldn't that be the responsibility of the Youth in Crisis people?"

Francesca's red lips turned up with a touch of amusement. He must look like a damn deer in the headlights. "They do speak but not for long. Graham did it every year. And without bellyaching, I might add."

Liam grumbled under his breath and made another note to write a speech. This wasn't in their original agreement, but he could make concessions. Sleeping with him wasn't in their agreement either, but that had worked out splendidly. He would get something out of this. "Fine. I'll write a speech. But you'll have to go out to dinner with me tonight then."

"Why?"

Liam leaned across the desk, his most seductive gaze focused on her. "Because I'm going to ply you with sushi and expensive sake, and once you're drunk, I'm going to…talk you into letting me off the hook or writing the speech for me."

Francesca laughed. "I'm no speechwriter. But you do have several in your employ. I suggest you bribe them instead."

That wasn't a bad idea. Being a media mogul had its perks. If only he could get one of his news anchors to deliver the speech, too. He made another note on his blotter. "Does that mean you don't want to have sushi with me tonight?"

"I do. And I will. But first I have a president to cajole

and a charity ball to throw." She got up from her chair and leaned down to give him a goodbye kiss.

This time, because they were alone, Liam wasn't about to let her get away with just a peck. When she leaned down to him, he quickly reached for her and tugged her waist to him. She stumbled in her heels and fell into his lap. He clamped his arms around her so she couldn't get away.

Before she could complain, his lips found hers. He really enjoyed kissing her. He enjoyed kissing women in general, but there was something about Francesca's lips that beckoned him to return to them as soon as he could. Maybe it was the way she clung to him. Or the soft sighs and moans against his mouth. Maybe it was the taste of her—like a sweet, creamy sip of coffee. But he couldn't get enough of her.

Francesca indulged him for as long as she could, then pulled away. "I've got to get to work," she insisted, untangling herself from his arms. She straightened her skirt and rubbed her fingers along the edge of her lips to check for smeared lipstick.

"You look beautiful," he assured her. And she did. Dressed up, not dressed at all, perfectly styled or fresh from bed. He liked it all.

Liam wanted to tug her into his lap again and maybe make better use of his desk than he had since he'd moved into this office. But Francesca wouldn't hear of it—he could tell. As it was, that kiss guaranteed she would be on his mind all day. He probably wouldn't be able to focus on anything until after dinner, when he could get his hands on her again. But it had been worth it.

"You can flatter me all you want, but you're not getting out of this speech, Liam." She pulled away and sauntered out of his office, closing his door behind her.

Liam sat in his chair for a moment after she left. If he breathed deeply, the scent of her rose perfume still lingered in his office. Was there anything about this woman he didn't like?

He thought for a moment, then shook his head. Not yet. He'd been physically attracted to her the moment he laid eyes on her, but getting to know her had made the attraction that much stronger. She was beautiful. And smart. And thoughtful.

He picked up the coffee she'd brought him and took another sip. Her flaring temper could be a handful to deal with, but there were two sides to that passionate coin and he was certainly enjoying the other half at the moment.

The situation Aunt Beatrice had forced him into was unfortunate. But he couldn't regret asking Francesca to be his fiancée. Drawing her into this circus wasn't fair, but she was the right woman for the job. He couldn't imagine it going nearly as well with any of the women in his address book.

He liked being around Francesca. Working with her last week had been nice. Liam had gotten very comfortable having Francesca around, and that was saying a lot. He'd dated his share of women, never for more than a few months at a time. But he had boundaries. He very rarely had them over to his house and if he did, it wasn't overnight. They didn't meet any of his family or at least hadn't gotten to a point in the relationship where he thought it would be appropriate.

And he absolutely never brought them into his workplace. His romantic life and his work were two wires that never crossed. He usually didn't date at work, Francesca being a notable exception. He even tried to date outside the business. It took a bit of effort when you lived in D.C. not to date someone in media or politics—his usual circles—but he liked it that way. Usually.

Francesca was changing everything. This fake engagement was growing into something else with every passing moment. He didn't just want Francesca to come to his house; he also wanted her to help him decorate it. He liked starting his mornings chatting with her over coffee in his office or at her kitchen table. She may not have met his family yet, but if Aunt Beatrice had anything to say about it, she would—and soon. If the engagement went on for long, maybe he could convince his mother and sister to come to D.C. for a visit. He actually liked the idea of introducing them. He was certain his sister would really like Francesca.

All his rules were being broken. Stomped on with a red stiletto was more like it.

Normally, that would make Liam cringe. This woman he'd lassoed and pulled into his life was blurring all his boundaries. And he liked it.

A gentle rap at the door made him look up from their engagement photo. "Yes?"

Jessica came in, a couple of files stacked in her arms. "Good morning, sir."

"Good morning, Jessica."

She smiled as she approached his desk. "You're looking quite chipper this morning. Love looks good on you, sir. As does Ms. Orr's lipstick."

Liam grinned sheepishly and got up to look in the mirror over the minibar. He spotted a touch of reddish-pink lipstick, which he quickly wiped off. "Thanks, Jessica. She would've let me walk around like this all day, I bet."

"Of course. I've got those things you asked for this morning." Jessica set the stack of paperwork on his desk. "Last month's ratings numbers for the 5:00 to 7:00 p.m. weekday time slots, the budget breakout for the gala this weekend and the copy of *Italian for Idiots* you asked me to order came in from Amazon."

"Excellent. Thank you, Jessica. I've got a meeting with the CFO today, right?"

"At four."

Liam nodded. "Would you call and make reservations for Francesca and me at that nice sushi place in Dupont Circle? At six? I should be done with my meeting by then."

"I'll take care of it. Anything else?"

"That should do it for now."

When Jessica turned to leave, Liam thought of something. "Wait, one more thing. I'd like to send something to Francesca. An unexpected gift. Any suggestions?"

His secretary thought for a moment. "Well, for most men, I would suggest flowers or candy."

"Am I not most men?"

"Not at all, sir."

At least she was honest. "Then what would you recommend for the smaller minority of men?"

"Perhaps something for the gala this weekend? Do you know what dress she's wearing? Maybe something sparkly to go with it?"

Liam seemed to remember her saying something about that yesterday. That she had to go find a dress, but she didn't know when she would have the time. Perhaps he could help with that. Aunt Beatrice had the personal shoppers from Saks Fifth Avenue and Neiman Marcus come to her when she was choosing an outfit for an event. His aunt rarely left her mansion anymore.

"Check Ms. Orr's calendar for tomorrow afternoon and move anything she has to another time. Then call Neiman Marcus and have them send over a personal shopper."

"They'll need her size, colors and any other preferences."

Liam wrote down a few things on a Post-it note and handed it to her. "This is a fairly solid guess on her size, although tell them to bring a few things larger and smaller in case I'm wrong. I want the whole outfit, so shoes too. She wears an eight." He'd seen the label on her shoe as he'd carried her from the engagement party.

"Anything else, sir?"

"Yes. I want her to be the most stunning woman there. She is gorgeous on her own, but I'd like her to have a dress almost as beautiful as she is. And as such, let them know there's no price limit."

Eight

Liam had wanted to escort Francesca to the gala, but she'd insisted she had to go early and that she would just meet him there. He anticipated that she would be running around for most of the evening. That meant loitering on his own. Normally that wouldn't bother him, but lately being separated from Francesca brought on an awkward tightness in his chest. The only thing that would cure it was holding her in his arms.

As he walked through the front doors of the hotel's grand ballroom, he was greeted by the sound of a ten-piece orchestra accompanied by the dull roar of several hundred people mingling. The light was dim, but his eyes quickly became accustomed to it. He searched around the room for Francesca, but he began to think it was a lost cause. She was a needle in a haystack.

Despite the fact that he'd paid for the outfit she had chosen for tonight, he had no idea what she would be wearing. She had been exceedingly pleased with the gift and had thanked him in several ways over the past week, but the only details she would share was that it was a Marchesa and "*molto bellisima*."

Then the crowds parted near the bar and he saw her. There was no mistaking this needle in any size haystack. The personal shopper from the department store had certainly taken Liam's requests into consideration. Francesca was the most stunning woman in the room tonight. He didn't even have to look around to check. He knew it in his gut.

The gown was black and gray with a swirling design. It was off the shoulder and clung to each curve all the way to the knee, where it fanned out into a delicate cascade of black marabou feathers. Her breasts were tastefully showcased by the neckline of the gown, which was trimmed with more feathers—there wasn't so much showing as to make him jealous of other men looking at her, but it was enough to make *him* notice. Her hair was swept up, making her neck look impossibly long and ready for his kisses. Her only jewelry was a pair of sparkling diamond dangles at her ears and a bracelet on one wrist.

When she turned to speak to someone, he noticed the feathers continued into a short train that draped behind her. It was grand, elegant and extremely sexy. And the best part was that *his* fiancée was wearing it.

He'd tried not to think too much of her that way. It implied more than there was between them, but he felt a surge of territoriality rush through him when she started talking to another man. He had the urge to rush to her, kiss her senseless and stake his claim before anyone got any ideas.

Then she held up her hand to show off her engagement ring. Even across the room, he could see the massive gem sparkle as her hand turned and she smiled. At long last, she radiated joy like a future bride should. The man said a few things, then they parted ways and she started walking in his direction.

The second her eyes met his, she stopped in her tracks. With a seductive grin curling her ruby lips, she held out her arms to showcase the gown and did a little turn for him. Lord, he thought, curling his hands into fists at his side. It was even more incredible from the back, where it dipped low to showcase her flawless, tanned skin.

Liam closed the gap between them as fast as he could without running across the ballroom. Up close, the dress sparkled as the lights hit little crystals sprinkled across the fabric, but it didn't shine as radiantly as she did.

"What do you think? Did I spend your money wisely?"

Not caring if he ruined the look she'd so carefully crafted, he leaned down and kissed her. He couldn't help it.

When he pulled away, Francesca smiled. "I guess so."

"Incredible," he said.

"Thank you for buying it for me. Having the woman from the department store just show up with gowns was perfect. I felt like I was an Oscar nominee with designers fighting for me to wear their looks on the red carpet."

"Hollywood is all the poorer for you not being on the big screen."

"Oh, stop," she said, smacking him lightly on the arm. "There's no one around to hear us, so you don't have to lay it on so thick."

Liam shook his head. "I mean every word. It wouldn't matter if we were all alone. I'd say the same thing. Of course, I'd be saying it as I unzipped you from the gown."

Francesca smiled and slipped her arm through his. "Let me show you where we're sitting. People are still milling around the silent auction tables, but the event should be starting shortly. You'll give your speech after the video plays about the youth facilities."

The speech. He'd almost forgotten about that weight dragging him down when he saw her looking so stunning. "Hooray," he said flatly.

"Did you bring it?"

He patted his lapel. "Got it right here. And I wrote it myself, I might add. No bribery was involved."

"I'm looking forward to hearing it."

They approached a round banquet table front and center, just beside the steps that led up to the stage. He helped her into her seat and took his own just as the orchestra music increased in intensity and the lights on the stage shifted to indicate the program was about to start.

Salads were brought to every place setting as the director of Youth in Crisis welcomed everyone and introduced the short video about their program.

Liam could only pick at his salad. With every minute of the video that went by, he felt more and more nauseated by the idea of speaking to three hundred people.

When the credits started rolling, Francesca sought out his hand and squeezed it gently. "It's time," she said, looking over to him. "You'll do great."

Liam took a large sip of wine and got up from the table. He made his way to the stairs and up onto the stage, where he was bathed in blinding white lights. He reached in his pocket for his speech, adjusted the microphone and tried to keep the frantic beating of his heart from being audible to the crowd. It was now or never.

"Thank you and welcome, everyone, to the eighth annual Youth in Crisis charity gala. As some of you may know, I recently bought the ANS network, which has a longstanding commitment to this organization. It's a partnership I'm proud of, and there are many people who work hard to make it possible."

He looked down in front of the podium, where he could see Francesca's dim silhouette. Her excited expression fueled his courage to continue. His heart seemed to slow and the subtle shaking of his hands subsided. He just might make it through the speech with her sitting there, silently cheering him on.

"First, I would like to thank ANS's Executive Vice President of Community Outreach and organizer of tonight's grand event, my beautiful fiancée, Francesca Orr. For those of you that don't know Francesca, she cares so deeply about this cause. With everything that has happened with our network in the past few months, there was some uncertainty about whether or not we could sponsor this event like we have for the past seven years.

"Well," he corrected, "I should say everyone *but* Francesca had some uncertainty. Come hell or high water, this gala would go on as far as she was concerned. The woman would give back her own salary to fund this event if she had to. I hope everyone rewards her determination by writing a big, fat check. I have agreed to match the largest private donation tonight as an engagement present for my bride, so feel free to stick it to me for a good cause."

The crowd laughed and Liam felt his confidence

boost. He shuffled to the next index card, gave Francesca a wink and continued in his bid to get the attendees to part with their money.

Francesca loved her dress. She really did. But after a long night, she was just as happy to change into a breezy slip dress and zip the gown into the garment bag she'd brought with her to the hotel. She couldn't stuff all those feathers into her little BMW and drive around. With that done, she stepped into the comfortable black flats she'd stashed away with her change of clothes and sighed in relief. Not only did her feet feel better, but the gala was a roaring success and—more important—it was over.

The ballroom was nearly empty by the time Liam found her gathering up the last of her things. "That was a very painful check to write," he said. "Remind me to kick Scarlet's fiancé for donating that much the next time I see him."

She smiled, standing and turning to look at him. His bow tie was undone, his collar unbuttoned. He managed to look casually sexy yet elegantly refined at the same time. "Daniel knows that it's for a good cause, as should you. And an excellent tax deduction," she added.

"It was worth it to see the look on your face when they announced how much money we raised."

"I can't believe it, really. We blew last year's donations out of the water. Everyone was buzzing about ANS tonight—and for a good reason." Francesca slipped her bag over her shoulder and took Liam's arm.

"It's about time," he said, leading them back to the front of the hotel where the party had been held. He approached the valet and handed him his ticket.

"I parked over there," she said, pointing to an area she didn't really want to walk to.

"We'll get your car in the morning," he said. "I want you to come home with me tonight."

That was an interesting development. Liam had yet to have her over to his place. She figured that it was a personal retreat for him. They'd always gone to her town house instead. And tonight, she really wished they were sticking with that arrangement. She had no change of clothes. She had what she had worn to the hotel and her dress. The designer gown, while fabulous, would look ridiculous in the morning.

"I don't have any clothes for tomorrow," she said.

"You won't need any," he replied with a wicked grin as the valet brought the car out.

Francesca gave up the fight. She was too exhausted after a long day to argue. They loaded her things into his convertible and she sat back in her seat, going with the flow. It wasn't until they reached his place that she perked up.

Liam had described where he lived as a town house, just a little bigger than hers, but he'd lied. As they pulled up the circular brick driveway, she found herself outside what looked like a two-story home. It was detached with a courtyard out front. Two stories of red brick with an elegantly arched front doorway and dormer windows on the roof.

"I thought you said you lived in a town house."

Liam shrugged and pulled the car into the attached garage. "It's close."

He came around the car and opened the door for her, escorting her toward a few steps leading up into the house. They entered through the kitchen. The cabinets were a stark white with glass fronts, set against stainless appliances and gray granite countertops. There wasn't a single dish in the sink and not a piece of mail sitting on the counter.

Liam took her garment bag and led her through to the front entryway, where he hung it in the closet. She set her bag containing the other items she'd needed tonight on the floor beside the door and wandered into the living room.

"It's a beautiful place," she said, walking over to the staircase and running her hand along the wood railing. The space had so much potential. It was a stunning home, but as he'd said before, it was probably just as it was when he'd moved in. White walls, hardwood floors, minimal furniture. There wasn't a single piece of art on the walls or personal item on a shelf. It looked like a model home or one stripped to sell. "But it does need a woman's touch," Francesca admitted.

"I told you I needed you to help me decorate."

"I didn't realize it would be such a large task."

Liam shrugged out of his tuxedo jacket and laid it across the arm of the couch. "Not what you were picturing?"

"I guess I was anticipating this place as more of a reflection of you. You seemed to guard it so fiercely that I thought coming into your home would give me some insight into who you are as a person."

"You don't see me in this place?"

Francesca glanced around one last time. "Not really. But I see what I should've expected to see. A house owned by someone too wrapped up in his work to make it a home. That speaks volumes about you, I think."

Liam's eyes narrowed at her. "My work is more important to me than the color of the walls."

"My work is important to me. But I make time for other things, too. I want to get married and have a family someday soon. When I do, I want not only a successful man, but also one that can take a step back from his job to enjoy family life. You'll burn out without that."

As Francesca said the words aloud, she realized she may have made a grave tactical error with Liam. He might not read much into what she'd just said, but it struck a painful chord with her. When she'd said the words, when she'd mentally envisioned getting married and having a family, she'd seen Liam in her mind. She had pictured this place filled with color and life and toddlers who looked like him.

She had let her heart slip away, piece by piece. It had happened so slowly over the past few weeks that she'd barely noticed the change until it was too late. Liam didn't know it, but Francesca had given her heart to him.

The man she could never really have.

It was unexpected, really. She was passionate about everything she did, but she knew from the beginning that this was business. There was no future for her with a man like Liam.

And yet she could see more now. Their future together was as crystal clear as the illuminated swimming pool she caught sight of from his living-room window.

"There's plenty of time for all that," he insisted.

This man, this workaholic, had so many layers to him she was anxious to explore. She knew there was more to him than he showed the world. The way he cared about his employees. The way he was handling the interview with Ariella. He had an attention to detail that went beyond just doing quality work. He was just as passionate about what he did as she was.

How could she not love that about him?

Love. Francesca swallowed hard and turned away from him to look out the window at his darkened yard and glowing turquoise pool. She couldn't look him in the eye with these kinds of thoughts in her mind. He'd know. And he could never know. Because it would never work between them.

Despite the future she could envision, there was a critical piece missing between them. He didn't love her. He wouldn't even be with her right now if it wasn't for his aunt and her demands. That was a bitter dose of reality to swallow, but the sooner she reminded herself of that, the better off she'd be when this "arrangement" came to an end.

"Would you like to see the upstairs?"

Pulling herself together, Francesca turned and nodded with a smile. Liam led the way up the stairs, showing her his home office, the guest room and finally, his bedroom.

Knowing they'd reached their final destination, she slipped out of her shoes and stepped onto the plush carpeting. She ran her hand over the soft, blue fabric of his duvet as she made her way to the window. She watched the glow of the city lighting the black night above the tree line, hiding any stars from her view of the sky. On a night like this, she really needed a sign to help her. Something to tell her she was making the right choices with Liam.

She reached for the *corno portafortuna* necklace she always wore and realized she'd taken it off tonight. It was in a pouch in her purse. She suddenly felt exposed without it, as though something could get through her protective armor without it. Looking down, she saw a rabbit sitting on Liam's front lawn. Before she could move, something startled it and the bunny shot across the yard, crossing her path.

A sign of disappointment to come.

Francesca took a deep breath and accepted the inevitable. She was in love with a man she couldn't have. She didn't need a rabbit to tell her disappointment was on the horizon.

The heat of Liam's body against her back was a bittersweet sensation. Just as her mind began to fight against it, her body leaned back into him. His bare chest met her back, his fingertips sliding beneath the thin straps of her dress to slide them off her shoulders.

The flimsy sundress slid down her body, leaving her completely naked with it gone. Liam's hands roamed across her exposed skin, hesitating at her hip.

"No panties?" he asked.

She hadn't worn any undergarments tonight. The dress was almost sheer and wouldn't allow for them. Besides, she knew how the night would end. "I can't have you ripping up all my nice lingerie," she said.

"That's very practical of you. I find that sexy. Everything about you just lures me in. I don't know that I'll ever be able to get away."

Francesca closed her eyes, glad her back was still to him. She wished he wouldn't talk that way sometimes. It was nice to hear, but it hurt to know it wasn't really true. The minute his aunt let him off the hook, this whole charade would end. At least now she wouldn't have to worry about faking the heartbreak when their engagement was called off. The tears she would shed on Ariella's shoulder would be authentic.

"Look at me," Liam whispered into her ear.

She turned in his arms, wishing away the start of tears in her eyes that had come too early. They weren't done just yet. She needed to make the most of her time with him.

When her gaze met his dark blue eyes, she felt herself fall into them. She wrapped her arms around his neck and stood on her toes to get closer. His lips found hers and she gave in completely. The feel of his hands on her body, his skin against hers, was an undeniable pleasure. She had to give in to it, even if it put her heart even more at risk.

They moved together, still clinging to one another as they slow-danced across the room to the bed. Her bare back hit the silky softness of the duvet a moment later. Liam wasted no time covering her body with his own.

As his lips and hands caressed her, Francesca noted a difference in his touch. The frenzied fire of their first encounters was gone, replaced with a leisurely, slow-burning passion. He seemed to be savoring every inch of her. At first, she wondered if maybe she'd had too much champagne tonight. That perhaps she was reading more into his pensive movements.

But when he filled her, every inch of his body was in contact with hers. He moved slowly over her, burying his face in her neck. She could feel his hot breath on her skin, the tension of each muscle in his body as it flexed against hers. When he groaned her name into her ear, it sent a shiver through her whole body.

Francesca wrapped her arms around his back and pulled him closer. She liked having him so near to her like this. It was a far cry from their wild, passionate encounter in her kitchen. Nothing like the times they'd come together over the past week. Something had changed, but she didn't know what it was. It felt like…

It felt like they were making love for the first time.

The thought made Francesca's heart stop for a hundredth of a second, but she couldn't dwell on it. Liam's lips found the sensitive flesh of her neck just as the movement of his hips against hers started building a delicious heat through her whole body. She clung to him, cradling his hips between her thighs as they rocked closer and closer to the edge.

When she reached her breaking point, she didn't cry out. There was only a gasp and a desperate, panting whisper of his name as her cheek pressed against his. His release was a growl against her throat, the intense thrashing of his body held to almost stillness by their tight grip on one another.

Instead of rolling away, he stayed just as he was. His body relaxed and his head came to rest at her breast. She brushed a damp strand of hair away from his forehead and pressed a kiss to his flushed skin.

As they drifted to sleep together, one of Francesca's last thoughts was that she was totally and completely lost in this man.

Nine

"Aunt Beatrice," Liam said, trying to sound upbeat.

After the maître d' had led Francesca and him to the table where the older woman was seated, she looked up at him and frowned. "Liam, do you ever wear a tie?"

He smiled, pleased he'd finally pushed her far enough to mention it. And now he got the joy of ignoring her question. He turned to his left and smiled. "This is my fiancée, Francesca Orr. Francesca, this is my great aunt, Beatrice Crowe."

Francesca let go of his hand long enough to reach out and gently shake hands with the Queen Bee. "It's lovely to meet you," she said.

Aunt Beatrice just nodded, looking over his fiancée with her critical eye. Liam was about to interrupt the inspection when she turned to him with as close to a smile on her face as she could manage. "She's more lovely in person than she is in her pictures, Liam."

He breathed a sigh of relief and pulled out Francesca's chair for her to sit. He hadn't been looking forward to this dinner. In fact, he'd deliberately not told Francesca about it until after the gala was wrapped up. She would just worry, and there wasn't any sense in it. His aunt would think and do as she pleased.

"I can't agree more," he said.

The first few courses of the meal were filled with polite, stiff pleasantries. His aunt delicately grilled Francesca about her family and where she came from. She was subtle, but Liam knew she was on a fishing expedition.

Francesca must've realized it also. "So what brings you to D.C.?" she asked, deflecting the conversation away from herself.

Liam swallowed his answer—that she was here to check up on him and their agreement.

"I'm speaking before a congressional committee tomorrow," Aunt Beatrice said, allowing the waiter to take away her plate.

She had mentioned that before, but Liam thought it had just been an excuse she'd made up. "What for?" he asked.

His aunt's lips twisted for a minute as she seemed to consider her words. "I'm speaking to a panel on federal funding for cancer treatment research."

Liam couldn't hide his frown. He also wasn't quite sure how to respond.

"Have you lost someone to cancer?" Francesca asked. Better that she ask the question because she had no real knowledge of her family history, as Liam should.

"Not yet," Beatrice said. "But the doctors give me

about three to six months. Just enough time to get my affairs in order before I take to my bed permanently."

Liam's glass of wine was suspended midair for a few moments before he set it back down. "What?" He couldn't have heard her correctly.

"I'm dying, Liam. I have stage four brain cancer and there's nothing they can do. Some of the treatments have shrunk the tumor and bought me a little more time, but a little more is all I'm going to get."

Unable to meet her eyes, his gaze strayed to her perfectly curled gray hair and he realized, for the first time, that it was a wig. How long had this been going on? "When did this happen? Why haven't you told anyone?"

At that, his aunt laughed. "Please, Liam. The sharks have been circling me for years. Do you really think I'm going to let them know it's close to feeding time?"

That was a true enough statement. The vultures had been lurking outside her mansion his whole life. This must be why she was so insistent on Liam marrying and taking over as head of the family. She knew the shoes needed to be filled quickly. She'd given him a year knowing she'd never live to see it come to fruition.

She'd been silently dealing with this for who knew how long. Worrying about her estate planning and altering her will even as she went for treatments and reeled from the aftereffects. "How can you go through this on your own? You need someone with you."

"I have someone with me. Henry has been by my side for more than forty years. He's held my hand through every treatment. Sat by me as I cried."

Henry. He'd never understood why her butler stayed around, even at his advanced age. Now perhaps he comprehended the truth. Neither of them had ever married.

They'd grown up in a time where they could never be together due to the wide social chasm between them, yet they were in love. Secretly, quietly making their lives together without anyone ever knowing it.

And now Henry was going to lose her. It made Liam's chest ache for the silent, patient man he'd known all his life.

"I don't know what to say, Aunt Beatrice. I'm so sorry."

"Is there anything we can do?" Francesca asked. Her hand sought out his under the table and squeezed gently for reassurance. He appreciated the support. Like her mere presence at his speech, knowing she was there made him feel stronger. As if he could handle anything.

"Actually, yes. I'd like the two of you to get married this weekend while I'm in town."

Anything but that.

"What?" Liam said, his tone sharper than he would've liked after everything they'd just discussed.

"I know our original agreement gave you a year, but I've taken a turn for the worse and I'm forced to move up the deadline. I want to ensure that you go through with it so I have enough time to have all the appropriate paperwork drawn up. I also want to see you married before I'm too much of an invalid to enjoy myself at the reception."

Francesca's hand tightened on his. It was never meant to go this far. He never expected something like this. "This weekend? It's Monday night. That's impossible."

"Nothing is impossible when you have enough money to make things happen. I'm staying at the Four Seasons while I'm here. I spoke to the manager this morning and he said they could accommodate a wedding and reception there this Friday evening. They have a lovely terrace for the ceremony and the Corcoran Ballroom is available for the reception."

Liam felt a lump in his throat form that no amount of water or swallowing would budge. He turned to look at Francesca. Her gaze was focused on her plate, her expression unreadable. She looked a little paler than usual, despite her olive complexion. Obviously, she was as pleased with this development as he was.

"I see no reason for you to wait any longer than necessary," his aunt continued, filling the silence at the table. "After all, you've found a lovely woman. By all accounts you two seem to be very much in love."

Her pointed tone left no doubt. His aunt had nailed them. He thought they had put on a good show. That it would be enough to pacify her until he could find the funding to buy her out. But he'd already heard from his accountant. The amount of money he needed was nearly impossible to secure, especially with the network in such a vulnerable place. They were looking at some other alternatives, but it would take time. Certainly longer that the few days they'd been given with her new deadline. That would take a miracle.

The Queen Bee was calling their bluff and he had too much riding on this hand to fold.

The waiter arrived then, setting their dessert selections in front of them. His aunt had never been much for sweets, but he noted a glimmer of pleasure in her eye as she looked down at the confection before her. He supposed that once you know you're going to die, there was no sense holding back on the things doctors told you were bad for you. What was the point?

Aunt Beatrice lifted a spoon of creamy chocolate

mousse and cheesecake to her mouth and closed her eyes from pleasure. Liam couldn't find the desire to touch his dessert. He'd lost his appetite.

"Don't make my mistakes, Liam. Life is too short to wait when you've found the person you want to spend your life with, I assure you."

At that, Francesca pulled her hand from his. He suddenly felt very alone in the moment without her touch to steady him. "We'll have to discuss it, Aunt Beatrice. Francesca's family is from California. There's a lot more to pull together than just booking a reception hall. But we'll be in touch."

Liam pushed away from the table to stand and Francesca followed suit.

"Aren't you going to finish your dessert?" his aunt asked, watching them get up.

"We've got a lot to sort out. I'm sorry, but we have to go."

His aunt took another bite, not terribly concerned by their hasty exit. "That's fine. I'll take it back to the hotel with me. Henry will enjoy it."

Liam's car pulled up outside Francesca's town house, but neither of them got out. It had been a silent drive from the restaurant. They must've both been in some kind of shock, although Francesca was certain they had different reasons for being struck mute.

When his aunt first started this, Liam had asked Francesca to be his fake fiancée. There was never even a mention that they would actually get married. He assured her it would never go that far. It seemed safe enough, even as she could feel herself slowly falling for him. Nothing would come of it, no matter how she felt. She wanted the kind of marriage Liam couldn't offer, but they only had an engagement.

Marrying Liam was a completely different matter.

Not just because it would never work out between them. But because a part of her wanted to marry him. She loved him. She wanted to be his bride. But not like this. She wanted to marry a man who loved her. Not because he had a metaphorical shotgun pointed at him.

When Liam killed the engine, she finally found the courage to speak. "What are we going to do?"

When he turned to her, Francesca could see the pain etched into his face. He was facing the loss of everything he'd worked for, and he wasn't the only one. She might not agree with Aunt Beatrice's methods, but she understood where the woman was coming from. Desperation made people do crazy things. This was an ugly situation for everyone involved.

"She called my bluff. I'm just going to have to call hers. Tomorrow I'm going to tell her that the engagement was a setup and that we're not getting married. I don't think she'll sell her stock to Wheeler. It's not what she wants. She's a woman accustomed to getting her way, but she's not vindictive." He ran his hand through his hair. "At least I don't think she is."

Francesca frowned. She didn't like the sound of that plan. She didn't exactly get a warm maternal feeling from the Crowe family matriarch. His aunt had nothing to lose. If she was willing to go so far as to force him into marriage, she had no doubt she'd follow through with her threat. "You can't risk it, Liam."

"What choice do I have? I can't ask you to really marry me. That wasn't a part of the deal. I never intended for it to go this far."

Neither did she, but life didn't always turn out the way you planned. "When would you get the balance of the stock?"

Liam sighed. "It doesn't matter. I'm not doing it. She's taken this way too far."

"Come on, Liam. Tell me."

"I have to be married for a year. The ANS stock would be an anniversary gift, she said."

A year. In the scheme of things it wasn't that long. But she'd managed to fall in love with Liam in only a few weeks. A year from now, how bad off would she be? That said, the damage was done. Maybe a year of matrimony would cure her of her romantic affliction. It might give her time to uncover all his flaws. It was possible she wouldn't be able to stand the sight of him by May of next year.

And even if she loved him even more…what choice did they have? Their network would be destroyed. They were both too invested in the company and the employees to let that happen. Her heart would heal eventually. It was a high price to pay but for a great reward.

"We have to get married," she said.

Liam's eyes widened. "No. Absolutely not."

She couldn't help the pout of her lower lip when he spoke so forcefully. She knew what he meant, but a part of her was instantly offended by his adamancy. "Is being married to me so terrible that you'd rather risk losing the network?"

Liam leaned in and took her face in both his hands. He tenderly kissed her before he spoke. "Not at all. I would be a very lucky man to marry you. For a year or twenty. But I'm not going to do that to you."

"*To* me?"

"Yes. I know you're a true believer. You want a marriage like your parents. I've seen your face light up when you talk about them and their relationship. I know that's not what I'm offering, so I won't ask you to compromise what you want, even for a year."

She couldn't tell him that *he* was what she wanted. If he thought for a moment that their arrangement had turned into anything more than a business deal, he would never agree to the marriage. He'd chosen her because he thought she could keep all of this in perspective. Knowing the truth would cost ANS everything.

Francesca clasped Liam's hands and drew them down into her lap. "I'm a big girl, Liam. I know what I'm doing."

"I can't ask you to." His brow furrowed with stress as he visibly fought to find another answer. They both knew there wasn't one.

"You are the right person to run ANS. No one else can get the network back on top the way you can. Ron Wheeler might as well carve up the company if you're not running it because the doors will be closed in a few months' time." She looked into his weary blue eyes so he would know how sincere she was. "It's just a year. Once you get your stock, we can go our separate ways."

"But what about your friends and family? It's one thing to lie about an engagement that gets broken off. But to actually get married? Can you look your father in the eye and tell him you love me before he walks you down the aisle?"

Francesca swallowed the lump in her throat. She was very close to both her parents. They could read her like a book, and even as a teenager she couldn't lie to them without getting caught. This would be hard, but she could do it because it was true. Just as long as they didn't ask if *he* loved *her*…

"Yes, I can."

"What about your town house? You'll have to move in with me."

That would sting. Francesca loved her town house. She could hardly imagine living anywhere else. But she saw the potential in Liam's place. She could make that place her own for a while. "I'll rent out my town house."

"You don't have to do that. It's only fair I cover your expenses to keep it up even while you're not living there."

"Don't you think your aunt would find it odd if the place was left vacant?"

"This is going to sound a little harsh, but if what she says is true, she won't be around long enough to know what we're doing. She will probably write the marriage stipulation into the stock agreement, but she can't dictate what you do with your real estate holdings."

Francesca wouldn't put it past her. She didn't seem like the kind of woman who missed anything. "I suppose we can worry about the details later." She waited a moment as she tried to process everything they'd talked about. "So…is it decided then? We're getting married this weekend?"

Liam sat back in his seat. He was silent for several long, awkward minutes. Francesca could only sit there and wait to see what he said. "I guess so."

"You're going to have to work on your enthusiasm pretty quickly," she noted. "We'll have to tell our families tonight so they have enough time to make travel arrangements."

He nodded, his hands gripping the steering wheel as

though someone might rip it away from him. "I'll have Jessica call Neiman's again and get you a bridal appointment. Can you call Ariella and Scarlet tomorrow? They did a good job on the engagement party. Maybe they can pull off a miracle of a wedding in three days."

"I can. They'll think we've lost our minds."

Liam chuckled bitterly. "We have. Let's go inside," he said.

They went into her town house, and Francesca went straight into the kitchen. She needed something to take the edge off and she had a nice merlot that would do the trick. "Wine?" she asked.

"Yes, thank you."

Liam followed her into the kitchen as she poured two large goblets of wine. When she handed him his glass, he looked curiously at her hand for a moment before he accepted it. "Can I see your ring for a minute?"

Francesca frowned, looking at it before slipping it off. "Is something wrong with it?" She hadn't noticed any missing stones or scratches. She'd tried really hard to take good care of the ring so she could return it to him in good shape when it was over.

"Not exactly." Liam looked at it for a moment before getting down on one knee on the tile floor.

Francesca's eyes widened as she watched him drop down. "What are you doing?"

"I asked you to be my fake fiancée. I never asked you to marry me. I thought I should."

"Liam, that isn't neces—"

"Francesca," he interrupted, reaching out to take her hand in his own. "You are a beautiful, caring and passionate woman. I know this isn't how either of us expected things to turn out. I also know this isn't what you've dreamed about since you were a little girl. But if you will be my bride for the next year, I promise to be the best husband I know how to be. Francesca Orr, will you marry me?"

She underestimated the impact that Liam's proposal would have on her. It wasn't real. It lacked all those critical promises of love and devotion for her whole life, but she couldn't help the rush of tears that came to her eyes. It felt real. She wanted it to be real.

All the emotions that had been building up inside her bubbled out at that moment. Embarrassed, she brought her hand up to cover her mouth and shook her head dismissively. "I'm sorry," she said. "Just ignore me. It's been a rough couple of weeks and I think it's catching up with me."

"That wasn't the reaction I was hoping for," he said with a reassuring smile.

Francesca took a deep breath and fanned her eyes. "I'm sorry. Yes, I will marry you."

Liam took the ring and slipped it back onto her finger. He rose to his feet, still holding her hand in his. His thumb gently brushed over her fingers as he brought her hand up to his lips and kissed it. "Thank you."

Francesca was surprised to see the faint shimmer of tears in his eyes as he thanked her. It wasn't love, but it was emotion. There was so much riding on this marriage. She had no doubt that he meant what he said. He would be as good a husband as he could be. At least, as good as he could be without actually being in love with his wife.

Liam pulled Francesca into his arms and hugged her fiercely against him. She tucked her head under his chin and gave in to the embrace. It felt good to just be held by the man she loved. As she'd said before, this had been an emotionally exhausting couple of weeks. The next year might prove to be just as big a challenge. But somehow, having Liam hold her made her feel like it just might work out okay.

It felt like he held her forever. When he finally pulled away, they both had their emotions in check and were ready to face whatever the next week might hold for them.

"It's official then," he said with a confident smile. "Let's call your parents."

Ten

Francesca's precious retreat was a mess. Her beautiful townhome was in a state of disarray with moving boxes and bubble wrap all over the place.

Liam was maintaining the payments on her town house, so the bigger pieces of furniture she didn't need could stay, but everything else was going to his place. She'd probably need these things over the next year. This wasn't some overnight trip or long weekend she was packing for. She was getting ready to move in with the man who would be her husband in a few days' time.

Her parents had taken it well. At least they'd seemed to. Who knew how long her father had ranted after they hung up the phone. Either way, they were making arrangements to fly to Washington on Thursday afternoon. Liam's mother was thrilled. She didn't hesitate to say how excited she was to come and meet Francesca. Liam's mother and sister were coming Friday morning.

Their story was that they were so in love they didn't want to wait another minute to be husband and wife. Incredibly romantic or unbelievably stupid, depending on how you looked at it. But no parent wanted their child to elope and miss their big day, no matter what they might think about the situation.

Things were coming together, although it didn't look like it from where she was sitting.

The doorbell rang and Francesca disentangled herself from a pile of her things to answer the door. She'd asked Ariella to come over for lunch, hoping she and Scarlet could pull off the wedding hat trick of the year.

When she pulled open the door, she found her friend on the doorstep, but Ariella didn't have the bright smile Francesca was expecting. Her brow was furrowed with concern, her teeth wearing at her bottom lip. She had faint gray circles under her eyes as though she hadn't slept. And, most uncharacteristic of all, her hair was pulled back into a sloppy ponytail. That wasn't the Ariella she knew at all.

"Are you okay?"

Ariella's weary green gaze met hers as she shook her head almost imperceptibly.

Alarmed, Francesca reached for her friend's hand and pulled her inside. She sat Ariella down on one of the overstuffed living-room chairs that wasn't buried in packing tape and cardboard. "I'll make tea," she said, turning to the kitchen.

"Is it too early for wine?" Ariella called out.

Probably, but if her friend needed wine, she'd serve it with breakfast. "Not at all. Red or white?"

"Yes," she responded with a chuckle.

At least she was able to laugh. That was a step in the

right direction. Francesca quickly poured two glasses of chardonnay, which seemed more of a brunch-appropriate wine, and carried them into the living room with a package of cookies under her arm.

It took several minutes and several sips before Ariella finally opened up. She set the glass on the coffee table and reached into her purse. Pulling out an ivory envelope, she handed it over to Francesca to read the contents.

Francesca quickly scanned over the letter, not quite sure if what she was reading could possibly be true.

"It's from my birth mother, Eleanor Albert," Ariella said after a moment, confirming the unbelievable thoughts Francesca was already having.

The letter didn't give many details. It was short and sweet, basically asking if Ariella would be willing to write her back and possibly meet when she was ready. There was nothing about the circumstances of the adoption, the president or where Eleanor had been the past twenty-five years. Nothing about the letter screamed authenticity aside from a curious address in Ireland where she was to write back.

"When did you get this?"

"It came yesterday afternoon. To my home address, which is private and almost no one knows. Most of my mail goes to the office. I must've read it a million times last night. I couldn't sleep." Despite her weary expression, there was a touch of excitement in Ariella's voice. She'd waited so long to find out about her birth mother. Yet she seemed hesitant about uncovering the truth.

Francesca understood. The truth wasn't always pretty. People didn't always live up to the fantasy you built up in your mind. Right now, Ariella's mother was like

Schrödinger's cat. Until she opened that box, Eleanor would remain both the fantasy mother Ariella had always imagined and the selfish, uncaring woman she'd feared. Was it better to fantasize or to know for certain?

Francesca looked at the envelope and shook her head. After everything that had happened in the past few months, she'd grown very suspicious and protective where Ariella was concerned. It wouldn't surprise her at all if a journalist was posing as her mother to get details for a story. But she hesitated to say it out loud. She didn't want to be the one to burst the small, tentative bubble building inside her friend.

"Go ahead and say it," Ariella urged.

Francesca frowned and handed the letter back over to her. "I'm excited for you. I know that not knowing about your birth parents has been like a missing puzzle piece in your life, even before the news about the president hit. This could be a step in the right direction for you. I hope it is. Just be careful about what you say until you're certain she's really your mother. And even then, you can't be sure she won't go to the press with her story if someone offers her money."

Ariella nodded, tucking the letter back in her purse. "I thought the same thing. I'm going to respond, but I'm definitely going to proceed with caution. I don't want to be the victim of a ruthless journalist."

"I'm sure the letter is real, but it can't hurt to be careful."

Ariella reached for her wineglass and then paused to look around the living room. "What's going on here?"

"I'm packing."

Ariella's nose wrinkled as she eyed the boxes stacked around. Her mind must've been too wrapped up in the letter to notice the mess before. "You're moving in with Liam? So soon?" she added.

"Yes."

"Wow," she said with a shake of her head. "You two certainly don't move slowly. Next thing you'll be telling me you're getting married next weekend."

Francesca bit her lip, not quite sure what to say to that.

Ariella's head snapped toward Francesca, her green eyes wide. "Tell me you're not getting married in a week and a half, Francesca?"

"We're not," she assured her. "We're getting married Friday."

Ariella swallowed a large sip of wine before she could spit it out. "It's Tuesday."

"I know."

"What is the rush with you two? Does one of you have an incurable disease?"

"Liam and I are both perfectly healthy." Francesca wasn't about to mention his aunt's incurable disease. That would lead to more questions than she wanted to answer. "We've just decided there is no sense in waiting. We're in love and we want to get married as soon as possible."

With a sigh, Ariella flopped back into her chair. "Scarlet is going to have a fit. Putting together a wedding in three days will be a nightmare."

"We have a venue," Francesca offered. She loved how she didn't even need to ask her friend if she would do the wedding. It was a foregone conclusion. Francesca wouldn't dare ask someone else. "The Four Seasons. We've reserved the terrace for the ceremony and the ballroom for the reception."

Ariella nodded, but Francesca knew she was deep in planning mode. "Good. That's the hardest part with a quick turnaround. We'll have to use the hotel caterer, so I'll need to get with them soon about the menu for the reception. Did you guys have anything in mind?"

Francesca was ashamed to admit she didn't. As a child, she'd always fantasized more about her marriage than her actual wedding. And even if she had dreamed of a princess dress and ten thousand pink roses for the ceremony, none of that seemed appropriate for this. She wanted to save those ideas for her real marriage. One that would last longer than a year.

"We will be happy with whatever you two can pull together on short notice. We don't have room to be picky."

Ariella reached into her purse and pulled out her planner. She used her phone for most things, but she'd told Francesca that weddings required paper and pen so she could see all the plans laid out. "Color or flower preferences?"

"Not really. Whatever is in season and readily available. I'm not a big fan of orange, but I could live with it."

Her friend looked up from her notebook and frowned. "Live with it? Honey, your wedding isn't supposed to be something you *live with* no matter how short the notice. Tell me what you want and I'll make it happen for you."

She could tell Ariella wasn't going to let her off the hook. She would give her friend her dream wedding no matter how much Francesca resisted. She put aside her reservations and closed her eyes. Fake or no, what did she envision for her wedding day with Liam? "Soft and romantic," she said. "Maybe white or pale-pink roses. Candlelight. Lace. A touch of sparkle."

Ariella wrote frantically in her book. "Do you like

gardenias? They're in season and smell wonderful. They'd go nicely with the roses. And maybe some hydrangeas and peonies."

"Okay," she said, quickly correcting herself when Ariella looked at her with another sharp gaze. "That all sounds beautiful. Thank you."

"What does your dress look like? It helps sometimes with the cake design."

Francesca swallowed hard. "My appointment is tomorrow morning."

"You don't have a dress," she said, her tone flat.

She'd been engaged less than two weeks. Why would she have a dress already? "I don't have anything but a groom and a ballroom, Ariella. That's why I need you. I will make sure that Liam and I show up appropriately attired. The rest of the details are up to you."

"Please give me something to work with here. I know you trust me, but I want you to get what you want, too."

"I've got to buy off the rack with no alterations, so I'm not going in with a certain thing in mind because it might not be possible. I'm hoping to find a strapless white gown with lace details. Maybe a little silver or crystal shimmer. I don't know how that would help with the cake. It doesn't have to be very complicated in design. I prefer white butter cream to fondant. Maybe a couple flowers. I just want it to taste good."

"Any preference in flavor?"

"Maybe a white or chocolate chip cake with pastry cream filling, like a cannoli. My mom would love that."

"I can do that," Ariella said, a smile finally lighting her face.

"And speaking of food, I did invite you over here for lunch. Are you hungry?"

Ariella shoved her notebook into her purse and stood up. "No time to eat, darling. I've got a wedding to put together."

Francesca followed her to the door and gave Ariella a huge hug. "Thank you for all your help with this. I know I haven't made anything easy on you two."

"Do you know how many bridezillas we usually have to work with? You're easy. Anyway, that's what friends do—pull off the impossible when necessary. It's only fair considering you just talked me off the proverbial ledge over this stuff with my birth mother. And taking on a huge job like this will take my mind off everything, especially that upcoming reunion show."

The president had agreed to Liam's show proposal right before the gala. Francesca had jumped from one event to the next, getting everything in place for the televised reunion. "You don't have to do it, you know. You can change your mind."

"No, I can't." Ariella smiled and stepped through the doorway. "I'll email you our preliminary plans and menus to look over tomorrow afternoon."

Francesca nodded and watched her friend walk to her car. It all seemed so surreal. She would be married in three days. Married. To a man she'd known less than a month. To a man she'd grown to love, but who she knew didn't feel the same way about her.

A deep ache of unease settled in her stomach. She'd first felt the sensation when the shock wore off and she realized they were getting married on a Friday. That was considered to be very bad luck. Italians never married on a Friday. Unfortunately, the hotel wasn't available any other day.

Francesca hadn't seen a single good omen since that

ladybug landed on Liam's shoulder. Marrying Liam was looking more and more like a bad idea. But there was nothing she could do about it now.

Liam clutched a thick envelope of paperwork and a sack of Thai takeout as he went up the stairs to Francesca's town house. He'd met with his lawyer today to go over some details for the marriage. Now he planned to help Francesca with some packing.

"Hello," he yelled as he came through the door.

"I'm upstairs," Francesca answered.

He shut the door behind him and surveyed the neat stacks of labeled and sealed boxes in the foyer. "I have dinner."

"I'll be right there."

Francesca came down the stairs a few minutes later. Her hair was in a ponytail. She was wearing a nicely fitted tank top and capris with sneakers. It was a very casual look for her and he liked it. He especially liked the flush that her hard work brought to her cheeks and the faint glisten of sweat across her chest. It reminded him of the day they met.

God, that felt like ages ago. Could it really have been only a few weeks? Now here he was, helping her pack and clutching a draft of their prenuptial agreement in his hands.

"I see you've been hard at work today."

She nodded and self-consciously ran her hands over her hair to smooth it. "I probably look horrible."

"Impossible," he said, leaning in to give her a quick kiss. "I picked up some Thai food on the way from the lawyer's office."

"Lawyer's office?" Francesca started for the kitchen and he followed behind her.

"Yes. I got a draft of the prenup ready for you to look over."

Francesca stopped dead in her tracks, plates from the cabinet in each hand. Her skin paled beneath her olive complexion. There was a sudden and unexpected hurt in her eyes, as though he'd slapped her without warning. She set down the plates and quickly turned to the refrigerator.

"Are you okay?" Liam frowned. Certainly she knew that with the size of both their estates they needed to put in some protective measures now that they were making their relationship legally binding.

"Yes, I'm fine," she said, but she didn't look at him. Instead, she opened the refrigerator door and searched for something. "What do you want to drink?"

"I don't care," he said. Liam put the food and paperwork on the counter and walked over to her. "You're upset about this. Why?"

"I'm not," she insisted with a dismissive shake of her head, but he could tell she was lying. "It just surprised me. We hadn't talked about it. But, of course, it makes sense. This is a business arrangement, not a love match."

The sharpness in her tone when she said "love match" sent up a red flag in Liam's mind. He wished he could have seen her expression when she said it, but she was digging through the refrigerator. Then again, maybe he didn't want to see it. He might find more than he planned for.

He'd chosen Francesca for this partly because he thought she could detach emotionally from things. After she walked away from the elevator, he thought she could handle this like a champ. Maybe he was wrong. They'd spent a lot of time together recently. They'd had dinner, talked for hours, made love.... It had felt very much like a real relationship. Perhaps she was having real feelings.

Francesca thrust a soda can at him and he took it from her. She spun on her heel and started digging in the take-out bag. "So what are the high points?" she asked, popping open a carton of noodles.

She would barely look at him. She was avoiding something. Maybe the truth of the situation was in her eyes, so she was shielding him from it. If she was feeling something for him, she didn't want him to know about it. So he decided not to press her on the subject right now and opted just to answer her question. "Everything that is yours stays yours. Everything that is mine stays mine."

She nodded, dumping some chicken onto her plate. "That sounds fairly sensible. Anything else?"

"My lawyer insisted on an elevator clause for you. I couldn't tell him it wasn't necessary since we only plan to be married for a year. He said he likes to put them in all his prenups, so I figured it was better for it to be more authentic anyway."

"What is an elevator clause?"

"In our case, it entitles you to a lump sum of money on our first anniversary and an additional sum every year of our marriage after that. The money goes in trust to you in lieu of an alimony agreement. The longer we stay married, the more you're given."

Francesca turned to him, her brow furrowed. "I don't want your money, Liam. That wasn't part of our agreement."

"I know, but I want you to have it. You've gone far

beyond what we originally discussed and you deserve it. I'm totally uprooting your life."

"How much?"

"Five million for the first year. Another million every year after that. Milestone anniversaries—tenth, twentieth, etc., earn another five million."

"Five million dollars for one year of marriage? That's ridiculous. I don't want anything to do with that."

"If we pull this off, I'm inheriting my aunt's entire estate and all her ANS stock. That's somewhere in the ballpark of two billion dollars. I'd gladly give you ten million if you wanted it. Why not take it?"

"Because it makes me look like a gold digger, Liam. It's bad enough that we're getting married knowing it's just for show to make your aunt happy. If people find out I walked away after a year with five million bucks in my pocket...I just..." She picked up her plate and dumped rice onto it with an angry thump of the spoon. "It makes me feel like some kind of a call girl."

"Whoa," Liam said, putting his hands up defensively. "Now back up here. If we were getting married because we were in love, we'd probably have the same prenuptial agreement. Why would that be any different?"

Francesca shook her head. "I don't know. It just feels wrong."

Liam took the plate from her hand and set it on the counter. He wrapped his arms around Francesca's waist and tugged her against him. When she continued to avoid his gaze, he hooked her chin with his finger and forced her face to turn up to him. He wanted her to hear every word he had to say. "No one is going to think you're a gold digger. You will have earned every penny of that money over the next year. And not," he clarified, "on your back. As my wife, you're like an on-call employee twenty-four hours a day for a year."

He could tell his explanation both helped and hurt his cause. It justified the money but reduced her to staff as opposed to a wife. And that wasn't true. She was more than that to him. But if she was having confusing feelings about their relationship, would telling her make it worse?

"This isn't just some business arrangement anymore, Francesca. We're getting married. It may not be for the reasons that other people get married, but the end result is the same. You didn't have to agree to do this for me or for the network, but you chose to anyway. You're… *important* to me. So I'm choosing to share some of the benefits with you. Not just because you've earned them or because you deserve them. And you do. But because I want to give the money to you. You can donate every dime to charity, if you'd like. But I want you to have it regardless."

That got through. Francesca's expression softened and she nodded in acceptance before burying her face in his chest. Liam clutched her tightly and pressed a kiss into the dark strands of her hair.

It wasn't until that moment that he realized what a large price they were both paying to save the network and protect his dream. The reward would be huge, but the emotional toll would be high.

Five million didn't seem like nearly enough to cover it.

Eleven

Liam stood at the entrance to the terrace where the ceremony would take place. As instructed, he was wearing a black tuxedo with a white dress shirt and white silk tie and vest. A few minutes earlier, Ariella had pinned a white gardenia to his lapel. He looked every bit the proper groom, even if he didn't feel quite like one.

Beyond the doors was possibly the greatest wedding ever assembled on such short notice. Rows of white chairs lined an aisle strewn with swirls of white and pink rose petals. Clusters of flowers and light pink tulle draping connected the rows. A small platform was constructed at the front to allow everyone a better view of the ceremony. A large archway of white roses and hydrangeas served as a backdrop and were the only thing blocking the view of the city and the sunset that would be lighting the sky precisely as they said their vows.

About an hour ago, Ariella had given him a sneak

peek of the ballroom where the reception would be. It seemed as if an army of people was working in there, getting everything set up. The walls were draped in white fabric with up-lighting that changed the colors of the room from white, to pink, to gray. Tables were covered with white and delicate pink linens with embroidered overlays. Centerpieces alternated between tall, silver candelabras dripping with flowers and strings of crystals and low, tightly packed clusters of flowers and thick, white candles in hurricane vases. In the corner was a six-tiered wedding cake. Each round tier was wrapped at the base with a band of Swarovski crystals. The cake was topped with a white and pink crystal-studded *C*.

It was beautiful. Elegant. And completely wasted on their wedding, he thought with a pang of guilt.

Nervous, and without a herd of groomsmen to buy him shots in the hotel bar, he'd opted to greet guests as they came through the door. The wedding party itself was small with no attendants, but there were nearly a hundred guests. It had been a lightning-quick turnaround with electronic RSVPs, but nearly everyone invited had said yes, even if just out of morbid curiosity. So far, no one had asked any tacky questions at the door, like when the baby was due, but he was certain talk was swirling around the crowd inside.

"Ten minutes," Scarlet reminded him as she brushed by him in her headset, a clipboard clutched to her chest.

Ten minutes. Liam swallowed hard and pasted the wedding-day smile back on his face. In less than a half hour, he would be legally bonded to Francesca with all his friends and family as witnesses. A month ago, he'd been celebrating his purchase of ANS and looking forward to the excitement of fulfilling his dream of running a major network. Now he was about to marry a virtual stranger to keep the dream from crumbling into a nightmare.

"Liam," a proper female voice called to him.

He looked up to see Aunt Beatrice rolling toward him in a wheelchair pushed by Henry. He knew she was sick, but seeing her in a wheelchair was startling. Surely she could still walk? He thought back to every time he'd seen her in the past month. She had already been seated whenever he arrived. On their last few visits, she hadn't so much as stood up or walked over to get something from her bag. Now he realized it was because she couldn't. She'd done well hiding it until now.

"Aunt Beatrice," he said with a smile, leaning down to plant a kiss on her cheek. "And Henry," he added, shaking the butler's hand. He had a new appreciation for the quiet, older man who had served and loved his aunt all these years. "Seats have been reserved for you both in the first row on the right."

Aunt Beatrice nodded, and Henry rolled them into the room. There wasn't a "congratulations" or a "last chance to back out" from her. She hadn't even bothered to question him about his and Francesca's relationship any longer. He supposed that even if they were faking it, as long as it was legally binding, she was getting her way. She probably figured that within a year, they'd fall for each other for real. Or she'd be dead and wouldn't care any longer.

"Liam," Ariella said, approaching him quietly from the side. "We have a problem."

He wasn't surprised. As quickly as this had come together, things were bound to go awry. "What is it?"

"Security has spotted an uninvited guest in the lobby heading this way."

Liam frowned. "Who? A reporter?"

"Sort of. Angelica Pierce. How would you like us to handle this?"

Oh. That was certainly cause for a bit of excitement, especially where Ariella was concerned because Angelica had been suspended for her possible involvement in the hacking scandal that had revealed Ariella as the president's secret daughter. "Don't do anything. She's liable to make a scene if we have her escorted out. Better just to let her come and act like it's not a big deal."

Ariella nodded. "Agreed." She turned away and muttered into her headset. "Five minutes," she added, before disappearing toward the room serving as a bridal suite.

Liam busied himself greeting other guests and tried not to worry about Angelica. He'd only met the woman in person once, and he got the distinct impression that she was a suck-up who would do anything to keep her job. Right now, she was suspended pending the results of Hayden Black's investigation, so he wasn't surprised she'd shown up today. She was here to make an appearance and kiss up to her boss and his new bride.

He hoped that was all she was up to. He knew for a fact that Hayden and his fiancée, Lucy Royall, were already inside. Lucy was Graham Boyle's stepdaughter and there was some bad blood between her and Angelica. With any luck, they would sit far apart and not cross paths the whole evening. But he wasn't feeling very lucky today.

That's when he saw her. "Angelica," he said with a smile, accepting the hug she offered. "So good to see you." He wanted to keep this evening together, so he wasn't about to let on that she was an unwelcome party crasher.

Angelica seemed very pleased by the warm welcome. She'd certainly dressed up for the occasion, looking radiant even, if not a touch heavier than she had been a few weeks ago. Her face was rounder and her purple dress was a bit snug. The stress of Hayden's investigation must have been catching up with her.

"I wouldn't miss this for the world. I just love weddings. And my boss's wedding is an especially important event. I wish you both great happiness together."

Liam smiled and thanked her, turning to the next guests approaching. It was his rival network's former star, Max Gray and his new bride, Cara. They'd been married in March and had just come back from their extended honeymoon in Australia. The two of them were practically beaming with love for each other, and Cara's dress showed the gentle swell of her pregnancy. She had started doing public relations for D.C. Affairs since leaving the White House, but he could tell that motherhood was her true calling. She was just glowing.

As they approached the door, they both stopped to watch Angelica go inside. Max's jaw dropped, his eyes widening. His field research had helped uncover the hacking scandal back in January. "What is she doing here?" he asked.

Liam shrugged. "Trying to make friends, I suppose. Did you two have a nice trip?"

"Amazing," Cara said. "We slept in late, ate great food, did some sightseeing. It was wonderful. Where are you and Francesca going on your honeymoon?"

That was a good question. "We don't have anything planned yet. Things moved so fast and work has been so busy, we haven't had a chance. We're hoping things will slow down soon and we'll have the opportunity to get away. Sounds like a trip to Australia is a great choice. I'll have to talk to you two about it more later."

Max and Cara went to their seats and the last few arriving guests followed them. Liam straightened his tie and took a deep breath as he saw Scarlet and another man in a suit heading toward him with determination and purpose.

"Okay, showtime. This is your officiant, Reverend Templeton. He will go down the aisle first, then you. We'll seat the parents, and then the bride will come down the aisle with her father. Are you ready, Liam?"

That was another good question. He was ready as he was ever going to be for a corporate, shotgun marriage of convenience. The only thing that made him feel better was that he'd get to spend the next year with a sexy spitfire who made his blood boil with passion and excitement.

"I am."

Francesca sat still as stone at her dressing table, letting her mother pin the large, white gardenia in her hair. Looking at herself in the mirror, she was the perfect image of a beautiful bride on her big day. Her shiny, black hair was twisted up into an intricate updo, the gardenia pinned just to the side. Her makeup was airbrushed and flawless. She'd found the perfect gown in her size without much trouble. Even with such a time crunch, everything had worked out just as it should. It was as though this wedding was meant to be.

Only it wasn't.

Her persistent stomachache had kept her from eating

too much at breakfast or lunch. She had a plate of fruit and crackers beside her that she would pick at from time to time, but it just made the feeling worse.

Not even a saltine cracker could cure the ache of impending doom. This wedding was a mistake. She knew it. But the part of her that loved Liam and cared for ANS and its employees was overpowering her common sense.

She took one last look at herself in the mirror and inhaled a deep breath to pull herself together. Now was not the time to fall apart. Not while her parents' concerned eyes were watching her.

Since her father had come in, he'd been sitting in the corner, scowling in his tuxedo. Honestly, he'd had the same look on his face since she had met them at the hotel the day before. There had been a moment when he first saw her in her gown that his expression had softened and tears came to his eyes, but it hadn't lasted long.

Francesca was pretty sure her own wary appearance hadn't helped. But there was nothing she could do about it. She had to save her smiles and energy for the wedding and reception.

"Are you okay, *bella?*" her mother asked. She was a tinier version of Francesca, with the same dark eyes and warm brown skin. Her thick, brown hair was pulled back into a bun, with elegant streaks of gray running through it like professionally added highlights. She was wearing a shimmering gray dress with a jacket. Ariella had pinned a pink and white rose corsage to her lapel earlier. Her father had one very similar on his tuxedo.

Francesca nodded and stood, straightening her gown. She'd hoped for and found a white, strapless gown; there had been many to choose from because that style was in fashion. This one had a lace overlay that went to the floor and was delicately embroidered in a pattern with silver beads, crystals and pearls down to the chapel train. What she liked best about it was the silver sash around her waist with a crystal embellishment in the center. It accented her hourglass figure and gave the dress a little something special.

"Why do you ask?" Francesca asked innocently.

"You just don't look as happy as I was expecting. Where is my beautiful, blushing bride?" Her mother reached up to gently caress her face.

She stopped fidgeting with the dress and smiled, gripping her mother's hand reassuringly. "Yes, Mama, I am fine. I'm just a little nervous."

"You should be, marrying a man you hardly know," her father snarled from the corner.

"Victor!" her mother scolded over her shoulder. "We discussed this. We did the same thing, didn't we? And aren't you happy thirty years later?"

He shrugged and slumped into his chair. This was one argument he would lose, and he knew it. But he didn't have to like it. Francesca could easily see where she got her own stubborn streak and fiery temper.

"Mama, could you give me that small hand mirror so I can see the back?"

Donatella handed her the silver mirror and Francesca held it so she could make sure everything looked okay. Satisfied, she laid it on the edge of the dresser, but it tipped with the heavy weight of the handle and fell to the floor with a crash.

"Oh, no," Francesca lamented, crouching down to pick up the shattered hand mirror. There were only a few slivers of the reflective surface left, the rest scattered on the floor. Slumping into her chair, she looked at the broken glass and shook her head. "Seven years bad luck," she said. "As though I needed another sign."

"Nonsense," her mother chided. "Your *nonna* filled your head with silliness when you were a child. This means nothing aside from having to sweep up and buy a new mirror. Your marriage will be whatever you make it. And if you believe in your heart that it is doomed before it starts, you'll be right. You must fill your heart and soul with joy, not fear, as you walk down that aisle, *bella*."

Francesca hoped her mother was right. She should ignore the signs and try to make the most of her year with Liam. It was all she was going to get so she shouldn't spend the precious time she had moping about losing him.

A gentle rap sounded at the door and Ariella stuck her head in. "Mrs. Orr, it's time for you to be seated. I'll be back for the bride and her father in just a moment." She gave Francesca a quick wink of encouragement as they slipped out of the room.

Now was the moment Francesca was dreading the most. Five minutes alone with her father without her mother to be the buffer. Hopefully she could distract him with idle conversation until Ariella returned.

"How do I look, Daddy?"

The large Irishman crossed his arms over his chest and admired her for a moment before he spoke. "Like the saddest, most beautiful bride I have ever seen."

Francesca frowned at him. How could he see into her so well? "I'm smiling. Why do you think I'm sad?"

"There's something in your eyes. Something isn't quite right about all this—I can tell."

"Don't be silly, Daddy."

Victor stood up and walked over to her. He helped

Francesca up from her seat and held her hand tightly. "Look me in the eye and tell me that you love him."

Francesca fixed her gaze on her father. If she really wanted to back out of this wedding, this was her chance. All she had to do was say the word and he would have her on a plane to California before Aunt Beatrice knew what hit her. But she couldn't do that. Wouldn't.

She had to answer him honestly, or he would know. He sensed a problem, but he was barking up the wrong tree. If he wanted the truth of the matter, he should be asking Liam these questions. Without blinking, she spoke sincere words to him. "Yes, I love Liam. Very much."

"And you want to marry him?"

She did. It was fast, but she had fallen hard for her fiancé. Her trepidation was in knowing that no matter how she felt about him, their marriage would be over this time next year. How could she walk down the aisle knowing their wedding was a pointless exercise? Yes, it would save ANS and make a dying woman happy, but Francesca herself would be crushed in the process.

"Yes, Daddy. I want to marry Liam."

His gaze moved over her face, looking for a thread to pull at to unravel the truth, but there was nothing to find.

Another knock at the door came and Ariella stepped in holding Francesca's bouquet.

"It's beautiful," Francesca said as she took the flowers and admired them. There were pink and white roses, white hydrangeas and tiny white stephanotis. She'd given Ariella very little direction on this wedding, but with the bouquet, at least, she'd hit the nail on the head. Everything else would likely be just as perfect.

"Did you expect anything less?" she said with a smile. "It's time."

Francesca's father took her by the arm and led them down the hallway to the terrace. When she got the cue, Ariella opened the doors. They stepped onto the balcony to the sound of music from a string quartet. A hundred people stood up from their seats and turned to look Francesca's way as they kicked through rose petals down the aisle.

She was almost halfway down the aisle when she finally got the nerve to look at Liam.

Francesca had avoided it because she didn't want to see the truth in his eyes. He would likely look nervous. Maybe even fearful for what he'd gotten himself into. There would be no tears of love and joy. He would not be beaming with pride after seeing the woman he adored looking more beautiful than ever before. She knew she would be disappointed. But she looked anyway.

When her gaze met his, she felt her stomach do a flip. He looked so incredibly handsome. She'd seen him in a tuxedo before, but there was something different about the way he looked tonight. It was the expression on his face. There wasn't love there, but she did see admiration. Unmasked attraction. Deep respect. He knew how big a sacrifice she was making for him and he appreciated it. He just didn't love her for it. Not the way she loved him.

Francesca had to remind herself to smile and not get lost in her thoughts as they took the last few steps to the ceremony platform.

The minister began the ceremony, and her father leaned in to kiss her before handing her over to Liam for good. She couldn't meet his eyes then. If he saw the panic and fear there, he'd drag her down the aisle while everyone watched in horror. Instead, she closed her eyes and leaned in to his kiss.

"I love you, Daddy."

"I love you, too."

At that, he put her hand in Liam's and they stepped up together to be married.

Francesca thought she would be okay until she had to take that first step and her knees turned soft. It was only Liam's firm, reassuring grasp that kept her upright. He guided her to the minister, her hand clasped tightly in his.

"I won't let you fall. We can do this," he whispered with a smile and a wink.

She nodded and squeezed his hand.

The ceremony began, but it was a blur to her. The minister spoke, she repeated her vows, they exchanged rings and the next thing she knew, she was kissing her husband in front of a hundred people.

The roar of applause and the cheers were like a slap in the face, snapping her back into reality. The minister presented them as Mr. and Mrs. Liam Crowe as they turned to the audience. She clung to Liam's arm as they walked back down the aisle together as husband and wife.

When they rounded the corner to exit the terrace, Ariella was waiting for them. She escorted them back to the bridal room to wait for pictures while the guests made their way to the ballroom for cocktails.

Francesca rested her bouquet on the dressing table beside the broken mirror and slumped into her chair.

It was done. They were married.

They still had to sign the official paperwork for the license, but that would arrive any second now.

She almost couldn't believe it. She felt numb, like she was walking through a dream wedding instead of one in real life. It had been a beautiful ceremony, but it wasn't how she imagined her wedding day would be. No matter how many different ways she had pictured her big day, there was always a common element.

She looked over at Liam. He eyed the champagne glasses for a moment before crossing the room to pick them up. He handed one to her and held out his own for a toast.

"One day of marriage done. Three hundred and sixty-four to go."

With a sigh, she took a deep draw from her champagne flute and closed her eyes before the tears threatened to spill over.

One critical thing was missing from her fantasy wedding: a man who loved and adored her more than anything else on earth. And that was the one thing Scarlet and Ariella hadn't been able to provide.

Twelve

Liam was worried about Francesca. As she'd walked down the aisle toward him, she was literally the most beautiful bride he'd ever seen. The white gown was quite flattering against the warm color of her skin and it fit her curves like a glove.

For a moment, it had all become a little too real. His breath had caught in his throat. His mouth had gone bone-dry. His heart had raced a thousand miles an hour in his chest. Francesca was about to be his wife. And in that instant, he'd wanted her to be in every sense of the word.

It was a strange feeling. One he hadn't experienced before. He'd been fond of a lot of women over the years. He genuinely liked and respected Francesca. That was probably as close to "love" as he'd ever gotten. Marriage hadn't crossed his mind yet. He assumed he would get to that point in his life eventually. The Queen Bee had just accelerated his schedule.

Liam wasn't sure if it was the flowers or the music. The way she looked in that dress or the happy tears of his mother. But he was committed to the moment. He was excited to marry Francesca. Maybe this year wouldn't be so bad. Maybe…maybe there could be more than just a business arrangement between them. A real relationship.

He was snapped back to reality by the stony expression on Francesca's face. There was no happy, bridal glow. No tears of joy. No smile of excitement. She didn't look outright unhappy; she was covering it well, but Liam knew she was on the edge. The reality of lying to all their friends and family must be weighing heavily on her. He understood. That was why he'd given her the option not to go through with the marriage. But she'd insisted. She wasn't the type of woman to go back on her word. She would choke it down and do what had to be done.

Since they'd left the bridal suite, she'd become like a robot. She smiled, she went through the motions, but her dark eyes were dead. He wasn't sure what would happen when she couldn't hold in her emotions any longer. But he knew it wouldn't be pretty.

Fortunately, they were able to lose themselves in the smiles, handshakes and hugs of the receiving line. After that, the reception should be fairly short. With little notice, Scarlet and Ariella had only been able to arrange a catered hors d'oeuvres and cocktail reception. No band or dancing, no five-course sit-down dinner. Just an hour or so of mingling and cake, and then everyone would be on their way. It should be fairly simple to get through it without drama.

The last few guests came through the line and Liam and Francesca were able to leave their stations. He put his arm around her waist and leaned into her. "Are you okay?" he whispered.

Her wary eyes looked to him and she nodded. "I'm just a little overwhelmed."

"Do you want me to get you a drink?"

"Yes," she said with emphasis. "Please."

Liam left her side to get them both something from the bar. He was returning with a glass in both hands when he caught an unwelcome sight out of the corner of his eye. Hayden Black and Angelica Pierce were chatting. No, that wasn't the right word. They were having a discussion that verged on heated, if Angelica's stiff posture and tight mouth were any indication. What was she thinking, having a conversation with the investigator out to prove she was guilty? This couldn't be good.

As far as Liam knew, Angelica hadn't been called to testify before the congressional committee about the hacking scandal. He assumed it was because Hayden hadn't been able to piece together the details of her involvement. Or at least, to prove it. The suspicion of her guilt was nothing Liam could act on. He needed hard evidence to fire her, and if Angelica was involved, she had been very, very careful. She wasn't stupid. She was a ruthless, cunning reporter willing to do nearly anything to get the big story. He appreciated her ambition. But not her moral code.

Secretly, he hoped Hayden would find what he needed. Liam was nervous running ANS with Angelica still in his employ. He needed a reason to cut her loose permanently.

Their discussion was getting a little more animated. Liam searched the room for Ariella and Scarlet, but he didn't see them or the security they'd hired. He might have to intervene on this situation himself. Francesca's drink would have to wait.

As Liam got closer to them, he could hear what they were saying a little better. They were trying to speak quietly, but their passions were getting the best of them. At least, Angelica's were. Hayden was always very calm and collected.

"I find it laughable that people seem to think you were behind this whole thing," Hayden said. "As though the peroxide-bleached brain cells you have left could plan something more intricate than what kind of shoes to wear with what outfit."

A flush of anger rose to Angelica's cheeks. Her eyes narrowed at Hayden. She didn't notice Liam approaching them because she was so focused on their argument. "You think you're so smart, Hayden, but I'm not going to fall for your tricks. Is calling me a dumb blonde the best you've got? I expected better of you. All men see is what women want them to see. The hair and the makeup and the clothes blind you to the truth. But don't let appearances fool you. We may have the same hair color, but I'm not sweet and pliable like your precious Lucy. I earned my place at the company. It wasn't because my stepfather owned the network."

Liam expected Hayden to take offense at the insults Angelica was levying at his fiancée, but it didn't seem to faze him. "Yes," he agreed, "but Lucy has something you'll never have no matter how hard you work or how many people you trample."

Angelica nearly snorted with contempt. "And what's that? The love of a man like you?"

"Nope. Her daddy's undying affection. She's the beautiful little girl he always wanted. The one he raised as his own. He bought her ponies and went to her ballet recitals. He got her a convertible on her sixteenth birthday. I bet it breaks his heart that he'll be in jail and can't walk Lucy down the aisle when we get married."

Angelica stiffened beside him, but she brushed off his words with a shrug of indifference. "So what? Her stepfather spoiled her. Am I supposed to be jealous of her for that?"

"No. But you might be jealous because he didn't have to bribe people to keep *Lucy* a secret. He wasn't embarrassed of her."

"I don't know what you're insinuating," she said slowly, although the tone of her voice said otherwise. It was cold and flat, issuing a silent warning to Hayden.

It made Liam wonder what they were really talking about. He'd heard that Lucy and Angelica hadn't gotten along, but Lucy had left ANS to work with Hayden before he took over. He certainly didn't know anything about Angelica's past or her family. Why did Lucy's relationship with Graham make Angelica so angry?

Hayden really seemed to know how to push her buttons. Was he rattling her cage for amusement or was he trying to get her to make a mistake? Liam turned to his left and spied the wedding videographer, a field cameraman from ANS. Perfect. He waived the man over.

"I want you to very quietly, subtly, record their conversation. She can't know you're taping them."

The camera man worked on ANS investigations and undercover stings, so he was likely more comfortable doing this than taping greetings for the bride and groom. He eased into the crowd, coming up from behind Angelica, partially hidden by the towering wedding cake beside them.

Liam watched Hayden's gaze fall on the video camera for an instant, then back to Angelica. They both knew this was their chance to catch her at something when she didn't expect it.

"Admit it, Angelica. All this hacking business had nothing to do with presidential scandals or career-launching headlines. It was just a high-profile distraction to get what you were really after. The truth is that you were trying to ruin him. Getting your revenge, at last."

Liam held his breath, waiting to see where this conversation might go when she thought no one else was watching.

"That's a ridiculous, unfounded accusation. Graham was a lousy boss with questionable ethics, but he was hardly a blip on my radar. I've got better things to do with my time than try to ruin someone like him. In time, they always ruin themselves."

"It's interesting you would say that. But I've got a stack of pictures that say otherwise. Pictures of you modified to remove your fancy hairdo and contact lenses. It made me think of something Rowena Tate told me. She mentioned that you reminded her of a troubled, unstable girl at her private school. The girl had always gloated about her rich father, but he never showed up for parent weekends. He just mailed a check."

"I didn't go to private school," Angelica said, her jaw clenched tighter with every word he said.

"I did a little research and found old school records showing her tuition was paid for by Graham Boyle. Isn't that odd? He's always told people he didn't have any children of his own. It must've been hard growing up knowing your father didn't want anything to do with you. That you were just a mistake that could be fixed with enough money. If it were me, I'd want revenge, too."

"Shut up, Hayden."

"He didn't even recognize you when you came to work at ANS, did he? Sure, you looked different, but a father should be able to recognize his own daughter, right? Then you had to sit back and watch him fawn over Lucy, a child that wasn't even his."

"I don't have to listen to your wild stories. You're obviously grasping at straws." She shook her head, turning to walk away from their discussion.

"The sad thing is that you went to all this trouble, ruined so many lives, and in the end, you failed."

Angelica stopped dead in her tracks. She swung back to him, her eyes wide and furious. "Oh, really? What makes you think this isn't exactly the way I planned it? Those fools they arrested, Brandon and Troy, will take the fall for the wiretaps. All the evidence shows that Marnie Salloway orchestrated it. Graham Boyle is going to rot in prison and his precious network will be destroyed before too long. It sounds pretty perfect to me. My only regret is that in the end, I couldn't find a way to get Lucy's hands dirty enough to send her to jail with dear old dad."

"But he didn't go to jail because he loved you and wanted to protect you. It was pure guilt."

"I don't need his love," she snapped. "I've gotten this far in life without it. What I did need was to see that bastard brought to his knees. And I got that."

Hayden smiled wide and turned toward the cameraman. "You get that, Tom?"

The videographer pulled away from his lens and nodded. "Every single word."

Angelica's jaw dropped open, her skin flushing crimson in anger. "You bastard!" she shrieked. "You deliberately set me up. If you think I'm going to let you ruin my career with no physical proof of my involvement with the hacking, you've got another think coming. Even with that tape, no one will believe you."

Hayden just shook his head. "I didn't have to ruin your career. Like you said, in time, people always ruin themselves. I just happened to get that moment on film. I'm pretty sure ANS will terminate you when I show them that tape. And the FBI and congressional committee will find it very interesting. Soon, people will start rolling on you to cut a better deal for themselves. There's no loyalty among criminals. You'll be wearing matching orange jumpsuits with your daddy in no time."

Graham Boyle was Angelica's father? Liam frowned in confusion but was jerked away from his thoughts when Angelica reared back and slapped Hayden. He barely reacted to the assault, simply shaking his head and looking at her with pity in his eyes. "It's a shame you wasted your whole life on this. I feel sorry for you."

By now, a large crowd of the wedding guests had gathered around the argument. More witnesses. The more people that gathered, the higher Angelica's blood pressure seemed to climb. "I don't want your pity," she spat.

Liam watched her fingertips curl and uncurl as she tried to keep control, but she was unraveling quickly. At last, she reached out, and before anyone could stop her, she grabbed a large fistful of wedding cake. Less than a second later, she flung it at Hayden, silencing him with a wet slap.

"What are you looking at?" she screamed at the crowd. She grabbed more cake in each hand and started launching it at the crowd. Buttercream icing flew through the air, pelting the wedding guests. They screamed and scattered. Liam checked to ensure Francesca, Aunt Beatrice and his mother were out of the line of fire, but Henry wasn't so lucky. He took a large piece of cake to the front of his suit. But he only laughed, scraping it off his shirt and taking it in stride. After forty years with Beatrice, flying cake was probably nothing.

Before Liam could turn to get help, two burly security officers rushed past him. Angelica's eyes went wild when she saw them. She started kicking and screaming when they tried to restrain her.

"Don't you touch me!" she howled. "Let me go!"

Liam could only watch in amazement as she wrenched herself from the men's grasp, only to stumble backward into the cake table. It turned over, taking Angelica and the cake with it. Angelica landed smack-dab in the middle of the towering confection, coating her from hair to rear in buttercream. She roared in anger, flailing as she tried to get up and couldn't. When she did stand again, it was only with the help of the guards gripping her upper arms.

On her feet, she was a dripping mess. Her perfectly curled blond hair was flat and greasy with white clumps of frosting. Icing was smeared across her face and all over her purple dress. She huffed and struggled in her captors' arms, but there was no use. They had her this time. At last, Angelica had gotten herself into a situation she couldn't weasel out of.

"You know," Hayden said, "looking like that, I'm surprised people didn't see the resemblance before."

Angelica immediately stilled and her face went as pale as the frosting. "I don't look anything like *her*."

"Oh, come on, *Madeline*. There's no sense lying anymore about who you really are."

The calm in her immediately vanished. "Never call me that name. Do you hear me? Never! Madeline Burch is dead. *Dead*. I am Angelica Pierce, you understand? Angelica Pierce!" she repeated, as though that might make it true.

Several people gasped in the crowd. Cara stood stock-still a few feet away with Max protectively at her side. "Rowena and I went to Woodlawn Academy with Madeline," she said before turning to Angelica. "We were right. It *is* you."

"You shut up," Angelica spat. "You don't know anything about me."

"You're right. I don't," Cara answered.

The guards then escorted a wildly thrashing Angelica—or *Madeline*—out of the ballroom. By now, the local police were likely on their way to take her into custody. First, for disorderly conduct and assault. Then, maybe, for her involvement in the hacking scandal. Either way, a scene like that was enough cause for Liam to terminate her from ANS for good.

"I'm sorry about the mess," Hayden said, wiping some cake from his face. "I never expected her to come talk to me. She was so confident that she had me beaten. I couldn't pass up the chance to put a crack in her facade, but I didn't realize she'd go nuclear. It ruined your reception. Just look at the cake."

Liam shrugged. Somehow knowing it wasn't his real

wedding made it easier to stomach. "Nailing Angelica is important. You have to take every opportunity you can get."

He walked with Hayden out of the ballroom to where a few police officers were waiting outside. They answered their questions and gave out their contact information. Hayden opted to go with them to the station, but Liam knew he needed to get back inside and salvage what was left of his wedding reception.

When Liam returned, people seemed to be milling around, at a loss for what to do with themselves. "Sorry about that, folks," he said, raising his hands to get everyone's attention. "Please stick around and enjoy the reception. I'm sad to say there won't be any cake, though." A few people chuckled and most awkwardly returned to nibbling and drinking as they had before the fight broke out.

Liam noticed the drinks he'd fetched from the bar still untouched on the table. He'd gotten wrapped up in the scene and had forgotten to take Francesca her champagne. He picked them back up and turned, looking for her. After all that, they'd need another round pretty quickly.

But she was nowhere to be found.

Frowning, he searched the ballroom, finally turning to a frazzled Ariella for help. "Have you seen the bride?" he asked.

"Not since I put her in a cab."

"A cab?" Liam frowned. "You mean she's left her own reception? Without me?"

Ariella bit her lip and nodded. "About ten minutes ago. Right about the time Angelica started bathing in wedding cake. She needed to get out of here."

Liam glanced around the mess of a ballroom. Scarlet was frantically informing staff of their cleanup duties. The guests were still standing around, but despite his assurances, they seemed unsure of whether they should stay. It was a wedding disaster.

He didn't blame Francesca one bit for leaving.

Francesca couldn't get out of her wedding dress fast enough. The corset-tight bodice made her feel like she couldn't breathe. It was all just too much.

Initially, she'd been relieved when Hayden and Angelica started making a scene. For the first time that day, every eye in the room wasn't on her. It was a blessed break. It was the first moment since she started down the aisle that she thought she might be able to let the facade of bridal bliss drop and regather herself.

And then the cake started flying.

Her *nonna* had never specifically mentioned that having her wedding cake flung across the room was bad luck, but Francesca was ready to make her own deduction about that. Their reception was a disaster. Their sham of a marriage would no doubt be a mess, too. It was just one more thing, one more blazing neon sign trying to point her in the right direction. She'd ignored all the other portents of bad luck. The fates had ensured this last one would be undeniable.

When she'd asked Ariella to get her a cab, her friend probably thought she was upset about having her reception ruined. The truth was that she just couldn't pretend anymore. If she'd had to be in that ballroom one more minute, she would have blown everything for Liam and ANS.

Now that she was back at Liam's place, in a pair of

jeans and a light sweater, she felt better and worse all at once. Boxes of her things still sat around the ground floor of his town house ready to be incorporated into her new life with him. But they might as well go back onto the moving truck.

She poured herself a glass of wine to calm her nerves and went upstairs to the master bedroom to repack. The only things of hers that had been put away were her clothes and personal effects for the bed and bath. Those could easily be rounded back up, and she intended to do it right now.

If she hurried, she would be sleeping in her own bed tonight. Not quite the wedding night everyone was expecting her to have.

She had one suitcase filled and zipped closed when she heard the front door open.

"Francesca?" Liam called.

"I'm upstairs," she answered and pulled another bag onto the bed. She was stuffing it with lingerie and pajamas when he came through the doorway of his bedroom.

Francesca tried not to think about how handsome he looked in his rumpled tuxedo. His tie was undone, his collar unbuttoned. She liked him tousled. Despite everything, she felt her body react to his presence. Her pulse started racing, and her skin tightened in anticipation of his touch. But thinking about how much she wanted Liam wouldn't help. It would make her want to stay. And she needed to go.

"What are you doing?" he asked. His voice wasn't raised. It was quiet and tired. They'd both had a long day and didn't need any more drama. But this had to happen tonight.

"I'm packing my things and moving back into my

place." Francesca shoved another few items into her bag and looked up. "Don't worry, I'll lie low until Aunt Beatrice leaves town on Monday, but then I'm calling the moving company to come get my stuff."

Liam took a few steps toward her. She could feel the magnetic pull of him grow stronger as he came closer. She wanted to bury her face in his lapel and forget about everything that was going wrong. But she couldn't.

"Why?"

Francesca put the last of her clothes into the bag and zipped it closed. She looked at the bag as she spoke to ensure she could get all the words out. "I'm sorry, Liam. I thought I could do this. But I just can't."

There was a pause before he answered, his voice a touch strained. "Do you want an annulment?"

She looked up at him and shook her head. "No. I'll remain legally married to you for the sake of the network. Hopefully that will be enough because I can't play house with you. It's too hard on…" Her voice started to falter as tears rushed to her eyes. She immediately turned from him before she gave away how she really felt. "It's too hard on my heart, Liam."

He took another step forward, but stopped short of reaching out to her. "What do you mean?"

Francesca took a deep breath. "I want more."

"More than the five million?"

At that, Francesca jerked her head up to meet his gaze. "You just don't get it, do you? I don't want your money. I never did. I have plenty of my own. I want the things that you can't give me. I want love. A real family. A marriage like my parents have. I want a man who cares for me more than anyone or anything."

She shook her head and hoisted the strap of the bag

over her shoulder. "This isn't your fault. You were right when you said I was a true believer. I am. But I've been lying to myself. First, I told myself that I could be with you and it would be fine. That I could spend the next year pretending. But I can't because I was stupid enough to fall for you. Then I kept hoping that maybe, just maybe, you would fall for me and this could become more than just a business arrangement. Silly, right?"

Liam reached out to her, but Francesca sidestepped him. "Don't," she said. "Just don't. I know you don't have feelings for me. Anything you say right now will make it worse."

She extended the handle of her suitcase and rolled it to the bedroom door.

"Francesca, wait."

She stopped and turned to him. This was the moment everything hinged on. If she was wrong and he did care for her, this was the time for him to say it. She looked into his dark blue eyes, hoping to see there the love she wanted so desperately. Etched into his pained expression was desperation and confusion. He didn't want her to go, but he didn't know how to ask her to stay.

"Liam, would you have ever considered marrying me if your aunt hadn't forced us into this situation? I mean, would you even have asked me on a date after what happened between us in the elevator? Honestly."

Liam frowned and shoved his hands into his pockets. "No, I probably wouldn't have."

At least they were both telling the truth now. Nodding, she turned away and hauled her luggage down the stairs. It was time for her to go home and pick up the pieces of her life.

Thirteen

Liam signed Angelica's termination paperwork and pushed the pages across his desk. He thought he would be happy to see this issue put to bed, but he wasn't. He was the most miserable newlywed in history.

For one thing, he hadn't seen the bride since their wedding night. It had been a long, lonely weekend without her there. He'd quickly grown accustomed to having her around. Now his town house felt cold and empty.

The office wasn't much better. Francesca didn't greet him first thing with coffee and a kiss. He wasn't even sure if she was at work today. He wanted to call her. Email her. But he knew he shouldn't. It would make it easier on her if he took a step back and let her have the space she needed. She deserved that much.

But he missed his wife.

How quickly she had become that in his mind. She was no longer his employee. She was his wife. There was no differentiation in his mind about the terms of their marriage. Their engagement may have been a ruse, but the wedding and the marriage felt real to him. Frighteningly real.

Liam had never given much thought to a wife and family, but the minute Francesca walked out the door, a hole formed in his chest. It was as though she'd ripped out his heart and taken it with her. All he was left with was the dull ache of longing for her.

That didn't feel fake to him.

Yes, he'd been pushed into the marriage to please his aunt. He had to admit that much to Francesca because it was true. But now that he was married to her, it felt right. It felt natural. He no longer cared about Aunt Beatrice's opinion on the matter. He…was in love with Francesca.

"I love my wife," he said out loud to his empty office. There was no one to hear him, but saying it had lifted a huge weight from his shoulders. Unfortunately, admitting the truth was just the first step.

How could he prove to Francesca that he really did love her? That this wasn't about the network or stock deals? There was no way for her to know for sure that he wasn't just playing nice for appearances.

The only way to convince her, the only sure path, would be to take the stock deal and the network woes off the table. If his aunt had no negotiating power over him, then he stayed married to Francesca because he wanted to, not just because he had to.

But to do that without risking the company would mean that he needed enough stock to control ANS without his aunt's shares. That seemed virtually impossible. Unless…

Liam grabbed his phone and leaped out from behind

his desk. He had to find Victor Orr before they returned to California. Francesca had mentioned they were staying on a few days to tour the Smithsonian, so if he had any luck, they were still in D.C.

It took two phone calls and a drive to their hotel in bumper-to-bumper traffic, but Liam was finally able to track down Francesca's parents. He was standing at the door, waiting for them to answer the buzzer, when he realized he didn't know exactly what he was going to say to them. He would have to admit the truth. And that would mean that a very large, angry Irishman might be beating him senseless within minutes for hurting his daughter.

Victor answered the door with a frown. Without speaking a word, he seemed to realize something was wrong. Why else would his new son-in-law show up alone just days after the wedding? He led Liam into their suite and gestured for him to sit down in one of the chairs in the living room.

He watched Liam through narrowed eyes for a few minutes before Liam gathered the nerve to speak.

"There are some things I need to tell you," Liam said.

"I'm sure there are." Victor leaned back in his chair, ready to listen.

Without knowing the best way to tell the story, Liam chose to start at the beginning. He began with the stock arrangement with his aunt, delicately skipping over the elevator debacle, and followed with Beatrice's later demand that he marry to keep control of the network.

"And my daughter agreed to go along with this phony engagement?"

"Yes, sir. She seemed hesitant at first, but apparently she saw a sign that she should do it. A ladybug."

Victor shook his head. "Her and those damned signs. She gets into more trouble that way. Married to a man she hardly knows because of a ladybug!"

"We never intended to go through with the marriage, but my aunt was adamant we do it now. She's ill and wanted to make sure we followed through. I told Francesca she didn't have to do it, but she insisted."

"She's stubborn like I am."

Liam chose not to touch that statement. "What neither of us realized was that we might actually fall for one another. On our wedding night, Francesca told me she had feelings for me that she knew weren't mutual and she couldn't go on that way."

"You just let her walk out like that?"

Liam frowned and looked down at his hands. "I didn't know what to tell her. I wasn't sure how I felt about everything. What was real between us and what was a fantasy? I didn't know."

"And now?"

"Now I know. I love your daughter, and I want to ask your permission to marry her."

"Son, you're already married."

"I know, but things are different now. I want to be married to her for real. I want to go to her and tell her how I feel, but I need your help. Francesca will never believe our marriage is anything more than a business deal as long as my aunt is holding the stock over my head. I can't afford to buy her out. But if I could get enough minority stockholder support, I might be able to get majority control without her shares."

Victor nodded. "I don't think I have enough, but I've got a good bit. So does my friend Jimmy Lang. Together, that might tip the scales. Let me make a call."

As Victor got up and headed into the bedroom, a simmer of hope started bubbling in Liam's gut. He really hoped that he could pull this off. He didn't want to go to Francesca and tell her he loved her if there were any suspicions about his motives. This was the only way.

"Good news," Victor said as he returned a few minutes later. "I spoke with Jimmy and did the math. Combined with yours, we have fifty-two percent of the company stock. Close, but we made it. Jimmy and I are both really excited about the direction you're taking the network, so we have no qualms about delegating our voting authority to you. So," he said, extending his hand to Liam, "congratulations. You're still running this network."

Liam leaped from his seat and excitedly shook his father-in-law's hand. "Thank you so much, sir."

Victor shrugged. "I didn't do it for you. I did it for my little girl. You have my consent to marry her, so get out of here and make it right between you two."

Liam's eyes widened as he nodded. There was no arguing with Victor Orr, even if he wanted to. "Thank you again," he said as he turned and bolted from their hotel suite.

As badly as he wanted to rush to find Francesca, he had one other stop to make. Fortunately, that stop was located in the same hotel.

Liam rang the doorbell at the penthouse suite and waited for Henry to answer the door. The older man arrived a few minutes later, welcoming Liam with the same smile and nod he'd always received.

"Come in, Liam. I don't believe she's expecting you this morning. We're packing to return to New York."

"I'm sorry to pop in unannounced, Henry, but I need to talk to my aunt. It's important."

Henry held out his hand to gesture toward the bedroom. Liam didn't wait for him, moving quickly across the carpet and around the corner.

Aunt Beatrice looked up as he charged in. She was sitting in her wheelchair folding her clothes. "Liam," she said. "I expected you to be off somewhere basking in wedded bliss."

"No, you didn't," he said, sitting on the edge of the bed beside her. "You and I have been playing a dangerous game that could end up doing nothing but hurting people."

She didn't bother acting offended by his insinuation. "I did what I thought was best for the family. And for you, despite what you might think."

"I know," Liam agreed. "And I came here to thank you."

That, at last, got a rise out of the Queen Bee. She sat up straight in her chair, her eyes narrowing at him in confusion. "Thank me?"

"Yes. If you hadn't forced me to get married, I might've let Francesca walk right out of my life. I love her. And I hope she stays married to me for forty years—not for the network, or because of your demands, but because I want us to grow old together. That said, I'm not going to let you control me any longer. I don't need your ANS stock or you holding it over my head. I now have enough backing to maintain control of ANS without your shares or your billions. I don't care about any inheritance."

Aunt Beatrice sat silently for a few minutes, absorbing his words. After a while, he began to wonder if she was mentally going over the new changes to her will. He didn't care. Cut him out. Cut him *loose*.

"Those," she said at last, "are the words of a man who can take charge of this family." Beatrice smiled softly to herself and placed a blouse in her suitcase. "It's what I've been waiting for. I never intended to sell my stock to Ron Wheeler. I just wanted to see you settled down, in control and happy with your place in life. Francesca is the right woman for you. I knew that just as certainly as I knew you two were pretending. In time, I figured things would work out between you. Once you both stopped fighting it. It's a shame I'll be dead before I can see you two genuinely happy together."

"You knew we were faking the relationship?"

"It takes a smart, observant person to head this family. Very little gets past me, even now. But it's okay. I'm sorry for meddling in your private life. Blackmail really isn't my forte, but I did what I thought I needed to for the good of you and the family. I'll call my stockbroker this afternoon and have the shares of ANS transferred to you."

"What? Now?" He had years and millions to pay off before he owned those shares outright.

"It's your wedding present. Most people don't give networks as gifts, but you're not the typical bride and groom."

Liam reached out and took his aunt's hand. It was something he rarely did; she wasn't very affectionate, but he was seeing the dents in her armor. Her illness was revealing the person inside that she kept hidden. "Thank you, Aunt Beatrice."

She turned her head, dismissing his sentiment with a wave of her hand, but he could see a moist shimmer in her eyes. "It will be thanks enough when you save that company and take over handling our motley crew of relatives when I'm gone."

"Do I really have to be executor of the estate?"

"Absolutely. And don't worry. Eventually, you will grow accustomed to the constant ass-kissing."

Francesca left ANS early. She'd been a self-imposed prisoner in her office all morning, afraid she'd run into Liam in the hallway. She had had a few days to sit at home alone, licking her wounds, but she wasn't ready to see him again. Especially knowing that everyone still expected them to be a happy, newly married couple.

After overhearing Jessica tell someone on the phone that Liam was out of the office, she figured this was her opportunity to escape.

She made it back to her town house without incident. Relieved, she dropped her purse on the coffee table, kicked off her shoes and went into the kitchen for a drink.

When Francesca rounded the corner and found Liam sitting at her kitchen table, she nearly leaped out of her skin. *"Oh, dio mio!"* She jumped, pressing her back against the counter and clutching her rapidly beating heart. "What the hell are you doing here, Liam? You scared me to death."

He looked a little sheepish as he stood up and came over to her. "I'm sorry. I didn't mean to scare you. I thought you'd notice my car out front. You gave me a key, so I figured I would wait around until you got home. When I called Jessica she told me you'd left."

"I gave you that key when we were going to be a happily married couple. Using it after everything that happened is a little creepy. Why are you here, anyway? We don't have anything to talk about."

Liam shook his head and came closer. She was able to catch of whiff of his cologne and her body immediately began responding to him. Apparently, it hadn't gotten the message about the breakup of their nonrelationship.

"We have a lot to talk about. Starting with how much I love you and how miserable I've been since you left."

Francesca started to argue with him and then stopped. *Did he just*... She couldn't have heard him right. "What did you say?"

Liam smiled, sending her heart fluttering at the sight. He was wearing a navy collared shirt that brought out the dark blue of his eyes as he closed in on her. She noticed a few weary lines around them. He looked a little tired and tense, but she had attributed that to the stress of running the network and the fiasco of their wedding.

Could it be that he was losing sleep over her?

He stopped just short of touching her, forcing her to look up at him. His hands closed over her upper arms, their warmth sinking deep into her bones. "I love you, Francesca. I'm in love with you."

As much as she wanted to melt into him, she couldn't let herself fall prey to him. She ignored the excited flutter of butterflies in her stomach and pulled back out of his grasp, watching him with wary eyes. "You didn't love me Friday night. You could've told me then and you didn't. You let me leave. And now you show up singing a different tune. What happened? Did your aunt find out? Trying a different tactic to keep the network?"

Liam swallowed hard, a flash of resignation in his eyes. "I thought you would say something like that.

Which is why it took me so long to come see you today. I had some important business to take care of."

Francesca crossed her arms defensively over her chest, but she didn't think it would do much good. Her armor where Liam was concerned had been permanently breached. "It's always business first with you."

"You're right. First, I had to go confess to your father."

Francesca's eyes grew wide with unexpected panic. "You told my father? Why? He's going to kill me. How could you do that without asking me?"

"Because I needed his help. And his blessing to marry you."

"It's a little late for that."

"It's never too late where an overprotective father is concerned. Not only did he give his permission, but he and his associate have pledged their stock to support me at ANS, giving me a majority share without my aunt."

Francesca tried to process what he was saying, but she kept getting hung up on what kind of conversation he'd had with her father when she wasn't there. "You don't need your aunt's stock anymore?"

"No."

That meant they didn't have to be married. "But you don't want an annulment?"

"Absolutely not." Liam crowded back into her space, closing the gap she'd put between them. "I have no intention of letting you out of my sight, or my bed, for the next forty years."

The butterflies in her gut went berserk. She brought her hand to her belly to calm them. "Wait. You love me. You want to stay married to me. And it has nothing to do with the network?"

Liam nodded. "Not a thing. I told my aunt this morning that I wasn't going to play along anymore. I didn't want you to think for a moment that I wasn't one hundred percent sincere in my love for you. This isn't about my aunt or the network or appearances. It's about you and me and the rest of our lives."

His arms snaked around her waist and this time, she didn't pull away. She molded herself against him and let out a small sigh of contentment at the feel of being in his arms again.

"I am in love with you, Francesca Crowe. I want to stay married to you until the day I die."

Her heart skipped a beat at the use of her married name. She hadn't heard anyone use it since the wedding. "I love you, too."

Liam dipped his head down to capture her lips with his own. This kiss—their first as two people in love—blew away all the others they'd shared before. Every nerve in her body lit up at his touch. She wrapped her arms around his neck to try and get closer to him, but it could never be close enough. She lost herself in the embrace, letting his strong arms keep her upright when her knees threatened to give way beneath her.

Pulling away after what felt like an eternity, he said breathlessly, "I want us to get married."

Francesca wrinkled her nose and put her palm gently against the stubble of his jaw. "*Mio caro,* we're already married."

"I know," he said with a devious smile. "But I want a do-over. With a tropical honeymoon. And this time, it will just be the two of us. No family, no pressure and especially no cake throwing."

Epilogue

Antigua, One Week Later

Francesca had no idea a vacation could be so perfect. With Ariella's televised reunion show coming up, they didn't have the luxury of taking a long honeymoon, but they did manage to sneak away for a long weekend in the Caribbean.

So far, they had sunbathed, swum in the ocean, dined on the best seafood she'd ever tasted and renewed their vows in a private white gazebo hovering over the water.

Their previous ceremony had been legally binding but tainted by his aunt's machinations and Angelica's tantrum. Their vow renewal had been just for them. A chance to say the words again and wholeheartedly mean it. Afterward, they drank champagne in their private bungalow and shared a tiny cake for two that no one could ruin.

Today they had planned a snorkeling trip in the morning, followed by marathon lovemaking and lots of luxurious naps. The snorkeling trip had been excellent. The water was crystal clear and a rainbow of fish was in abundance. They were on their way back to the bungalow when Francesca stopped and tugged at Liam's arm.

"Liam, stop. Look," Francesca said, pointing out the television mounted above the cantina bar.

It was the live coverage of Madeline Burch's arraignment. Before they left, the video of her confession had played repeatedly at every news outlet, with ANS breaking the story. The media had jumped on the tale about her involvement in the hacking scandal after both Brandon Ames and Troy Hall agreed to testify against her. The news of her double life was just the icing on the ratings cake.

For a moment, Francesca almost felt badly for Madeline. She looked awful. Orange was not her color. Going without her expensive hair coloring and extensions, she had mousy brown roots at the crown of her stringy, thin hair. Her last dose of Botox had faded away, as had her spray tan. Her colored contacts had been replaced with thick, prison-issued glasses. Several more pounds also had been added to her frame since their reception. There was no doubt that Angelica was Madeline Burch now.

"The news is out," Liam said as the news banner at the bottom changed. They couldn't hear what was being said on the television, but the words scrolling at the bottom announced the breaking news that investigator Hayden Black had testified that Madeline was Graham Boyle's secret, illegitimate daughter. Liam had told Francesca what he'd overheard during the argument at the reception, but her motivation for taking down Graham had been withheld from the press so far.

"Wow," Francesca said, shaking her head. "It's just so sad. And senseless. How many lives were ruined just so she could get back at Graham for the way he treated her?"

When she turned, Liam was pulling his phone out of his pocket. He had done well to unplug from the news world while they were on their honeymoon, but now that the news was out, all his journalistic buttons were being pushed.

He unlocked his screen and started typing something, and then he stopped. He pressed the power button and slipped the phone back into his pocket.

Francesca arched an eyebrow at him in surprise. "Really?" she asked.

"I am sure the network and my employees have this story well in hand. And even if they didn't, I am on my honeymoon. I couldn't care less about Graham Boyle's secret daughter."

He turned to face Francesca, snaked his arms around her waist and pulled her tightly against him. She melted into him, surprised to feel the firm heat of his desire pressed into her belly.

"Right now," he said with a wicked grin, "I'm more interested in making love to my wife."

* * * * *

COMING NEXT MONTH from Harlequin Desire®
AVAILABLE JUNE 4, 2013

#2233 SUNSET SEDUCTION
The Slades of Sunset Ranch
Charlene Sands
When the chance to jump into bed with longtime crush Lucas Slade comes along, Audrey Thomas can't help but seize it. Now the tricky part is to wrangle her way into the rich rancher's *heart*.

#2234 AFFAIRS OF STATE
Daughters of Power: The Capital
Jennifer Lewis
Can Ariella Winthrop—revealed as the secret love child of the U.S. president—find love with a royal prince whose family disapproves of her illegitimacy?

#2235 HIS FOR THE TAKING
Rich, Rugged Ranchers
Ann Major
It's been six years since Maddie Gray left town in disgrace. But now she's back, and wealthy rancher John Coleman can't stay away from the lover who once betrayed him.

#2236 TAMING THE LONE WOLFF
The Men of Wolff Mountain
Janice Maynard
Security expert Larkin Wolff lives by a code, but when he's hired to protect an innocent heiress, he's tempted to break all his rules and become *personally* involved with his client....

#2237 HOLLYWOOD HOUSE CALL
Jules Bennett
When an accident forces receptionist Callie Matthews to move in with her boss, her relationship with the sexy doctor becomes much less about business and *very* much about pleasure....

#2238 THE FIANCÉE CHARADE
The Pearl House
Fiona Brand
Faced with losing custody of her daughter, Gemma O'Neill will do anything—even pretend to be engaged to the man who fathered her child.

HDCNM0513

REQUEST YOUR FREE BOOKS!

2 FREE NOVELS PLUS 2 FREE GIFTS!

HARLEQUIN® *Desire*

ALWAYS POWERFUL, PASSIONATE AND PROVOCATIVE

YES! Please send me 2 FREE Harlequin Desire® novels and my 2 FREE gifts (gifts are worth about $10). After receiving them, if I don't wish to receive any more books, I can return the shipping statement marked "cancel." If I don't cancel, I will receive 6 brand-new novels every month and be billed just $4.55 per book in the U.S. or $4.99 per book in Canada. That's a savings of at least 13% off the cover price! It's quite a bargain! Shipping and handling is just 50¢ per book in the U.S. and 75¢ per book in Canada.* I understand that accepting the 2 free books and gifts places me under no obligation to buy anything. I can always return a shipment and cancel at any time. Even if I never buy another book, the two free books and gifts are mine to keep forever.

225/326 HDN F4ZC

Name	(PLEASE PRINT)	
Address		Apt. #
City	State/Prov.	Zip/Postal Code

Signature (if under 18, a parent or guardian must sign)

Mail to the **Harlequin® Reader Service:**
IN U.S.A.: P.O. Box 1867, Buffalo, NY 14240-1867
IN CANADA: P.O. Box 609, Fort Erie, Ontario L2A 5X3

Want to try two free books from another line?
Call 1-800-873-8635 or visit www.ReaderService.com.

* Terms and prices subject to change without notice. Prices do not include applicable taxes. Sales tax applicable in N.Y. Canadian residents will be charged applicable taxes. Offer not valid in Quebec. This offer is limited to one order per household. Not valid for current subscribers to Harlequin Desire books. All orders subject to credit approval. Credit or debit balances in a customer's account(s) may be offset by any other outstanding balance owed by or to the customer. Please allow 4 to 6 weeks for delivery. Offer available while quantities last.

Your Privacy—The Harlequin® Reader Service is committed to protecting your privacy. Our Privacy Policy is available online at www.ReaderService.com or upon request from the Harlequin Reader Service.

We make a portion of our mailing list available to reputable third parties that offer products we believe may interest you. If you prefer that we not exchange your name with third parties, or if you wish to clarify or modify your communication preferences, please visit us at www.ReaderService.com/consumerschoice or write to us at Harlequin Reader Service Preference Service, P.O. Box 9062, Buffalo, NY 14269. Include your complete name and address.

HD13R

SUNSET SEDUCTION

The latest installment of USA TODAY *bestselling author*

Charlene Sands's miniseries

THE SLADES OF SUNSET RANCH

All grown up, Audrey Faith Thomas seizes her chance to act on a teenage crush. Now she must face the consequences....

*U*sually not much unnerved Audrey Faith Thomas, except for the time when her big brother was bucked off Old Stormy at an Amarillo rodeo and broke his back.

Audrey shuddered at the memory and thanked the Almighty that Casey was alive and well and bossy as ever. But as she sat behind the wheel of her car, driving toward her fate, the fear coursing through her veins had nothing to do with her brother's disastrous five-second ride. This fear was much different. It made her want to turn her Chevy pickup truck around and go home to Reno and forget all about showing up at Sunset Ranch unannounced.

To face Lucas Slade.

The man she'd seduced and then abandoned in the middle of the night.

Audrey swallowed hard. She still couldn't believe what she'd done.

Last month, after an argument and a three week standoff with her brother, she'd ventured to his Lake Tahoe cabin to

HDEXP0513

make amends. He'd been right about the boyfriend she'd just dumped and she'd needed Casey's strong shoulder to cry on.

The last person she'd expected to find there was Luke Slade—the man she'd measured every other man against—sleeping in the guest room bed, *her bed*. Luke was the guy she'd crushed on during her teen years while traveling the rodeo circuit with Casey.

Seeing him had sent all rational thoughts flying out the window. This was her chance. She wouldn't let her prudish upbringing interfere with what she needed. When he rasped, "Come closer," in the darkened room, she'd taken that as an invitation to climb into bed with him, consequences be damned.

Well…she'd gotten a lot more than a shoulder to cry on, and it had been glorious.

Now she would finally come face-to-face with Luke. She'd confront him about the night they'd shared and confess her love for him, if it came down to that. She wondered what he thought about her abandoning him that night.

She would soon find out.

Find out what happens when Audrey and Luke reunite in

SUNSET SEDUCTION
by Charlene Sands.

Available June 2013 from Harlequin® Desire®
wherever books are sold!

HDEXPO513

Love the Harlequin book you just read?

Your opinion matters.

Review this book on your favorite book site, review site, blog or your own social media properties and share your opinion with other readers!

Be sure to connect with us at:
Harlequin.com/Newsletters
Facebook.com/HarlequinBooks
Twitter.com/HarlequinBooks

HARLEQUIN®

A *Romance* FOR EVERY MOOD™

Stay up-to-date on all your
romance-reading news with the
Harlequin Shopping Guide,
featuring bestselling authors, exciting new
miniseries, books to watch and more!

The newest issue will be delivered right to you
with our compliments! There are 4 each year.

Signing up is easy.

EMAIL

ShoppingGuide@Harlequin.ca

WRITE TO US

HARLEQUIN BOOKS
Attention: Customer Service Department
P.O. Box 9057, Buffalo, NY 14269-9057

OR PHONE

1-800-873-8635 in the United States
1-888-343-9777 in Canada

Please allow 4-6 weeks for delivery of the first issue by mail.